Zentangle®
UNDER THE SEA

Hannah Geddes

ARCTURUS

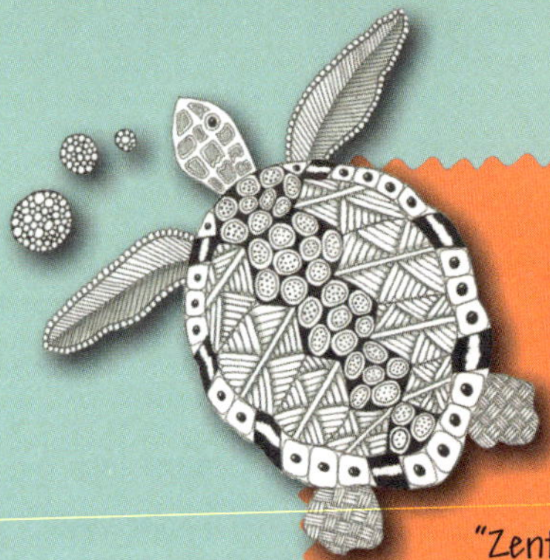

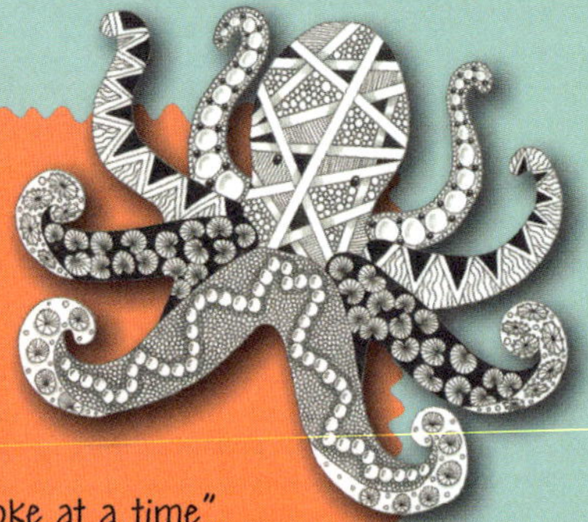

Acknowledgments

The Zentangle® method was created by Rick Roberts and Maria Thomas.

"Zentangle"®, the Zentangle logo, "Anything is possible one stroke at a time", "Bijou", "Certified Zentangle Teacher", "CZT"®, "Zentangle Apprentice"®, and "Zentomology" are trademarks, service marks, or certification marks of Rick Roberts, Maria Thomas, and/or Zentangle Inc.

BTL Joos (p48) by Sandy Bartholomew, Cruffle (p22) by Sandy Hunter, Henna Drum (p45) by Jane MacKugler (dicksallyjane.blogspot.co.uk), Hollibaugh (p31) by Molly Hollibaugh, Joy (p47) by Joyce Block, Lilypads (p37) and Lotus Pods (p36) by Margaret Bremmer, and Limpitz (p47) by Jo Newsham.

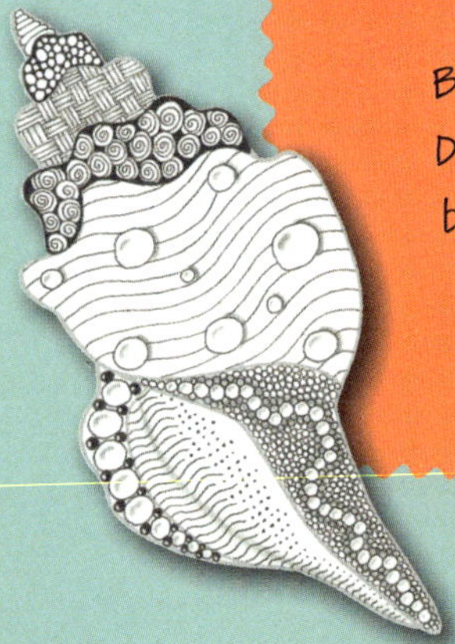

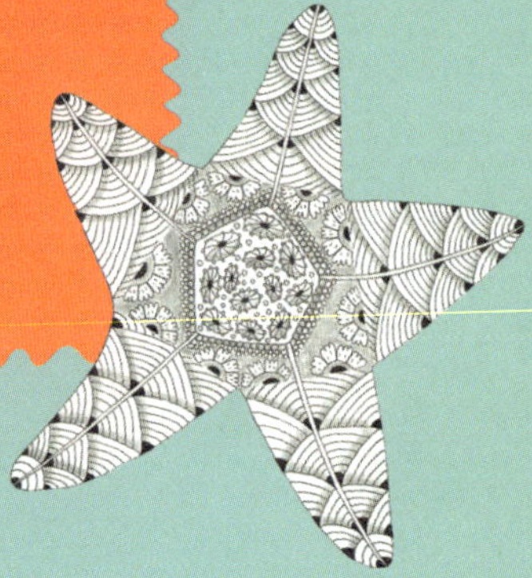

ARCTURUS

This edition published in 2016 by Arcturus Publishing Limited
26/27 Bickels Yard, 151–153 Bermondsey Street,
London SE1 3HA

Step-outs and Zentangle Inspired Artworks by Hannah Geddes
Text by Hannah Geddes and Frances Evans
Designed by Amy McSimpson
Edited by Frances Evans
Outline illustrations by Katy Jackson

ISBN: 978-1-78428-202-8
CH004937NT
Supplier 26, Date 0616 Print run 4990

Printed in China

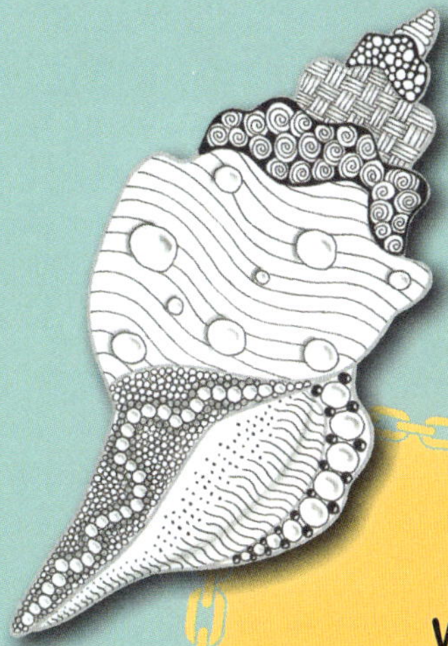

Contents

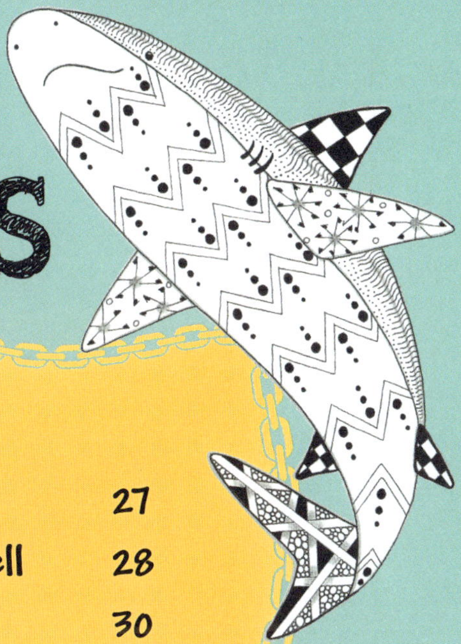

What is Zentangle? 4
Using Strings 6
Simple Tangles 7
Super Starfish 10
Onamato 12
Tagh 13
Fabulous Fish 14
Tangle Time! 16
Knightsbridge 18
Chartz 19
Tangled Turtle 20
Cruffle 22
Knase 23
Playful Dolphin 24
Printemps 26
Diva Dance 27
Beautiful Shell 28
Shattuck 30
Hollibaugh 31
Tangle Time! 32
Graceful Orca 34
Lotus Pods 36
Lilypads 37
Stealthy Shark 38
Meer 40
Quipple 41
Magical Octopus 42
Seaweed Tangles 44
Coral Tangles 46

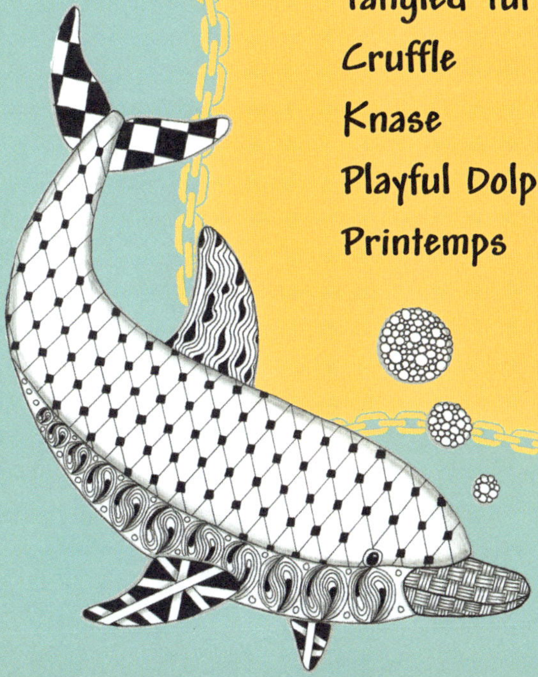

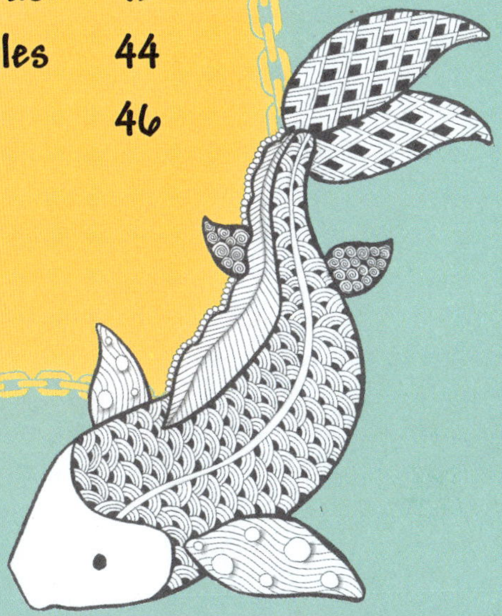

What is Zentangle?

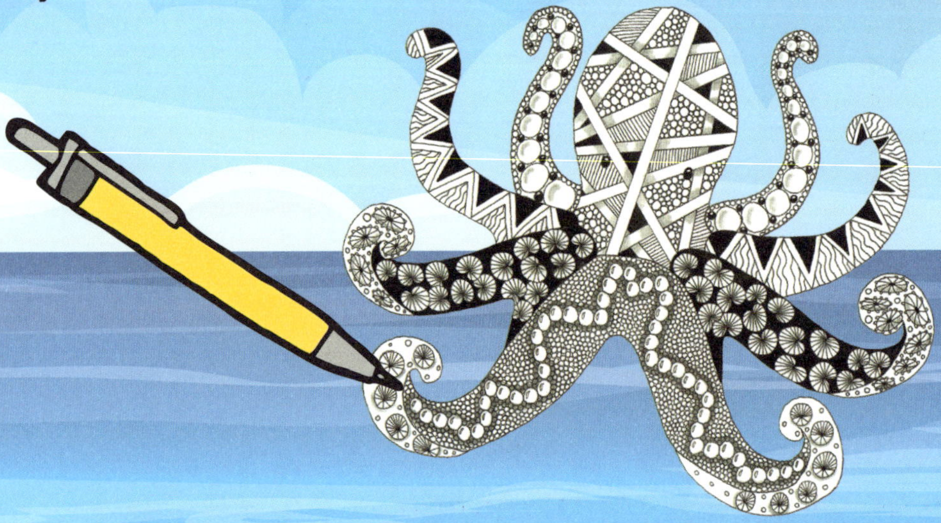

Zentangle is a drawing method created by Rick Roberts and Maria Thomas. It teaches you how to create beautiful pieces of art using simple patterns called tangles. Tangling is a really fun, relaxing way to get creative, and it brings out the artist in everyone. You can tangle wherever and whenever the mood takes you!

This book will show you how to draw 30 different tangles and use them to create incredible underwater artworks. Simply grab a pen and some paper, and take your tangles under the sea...

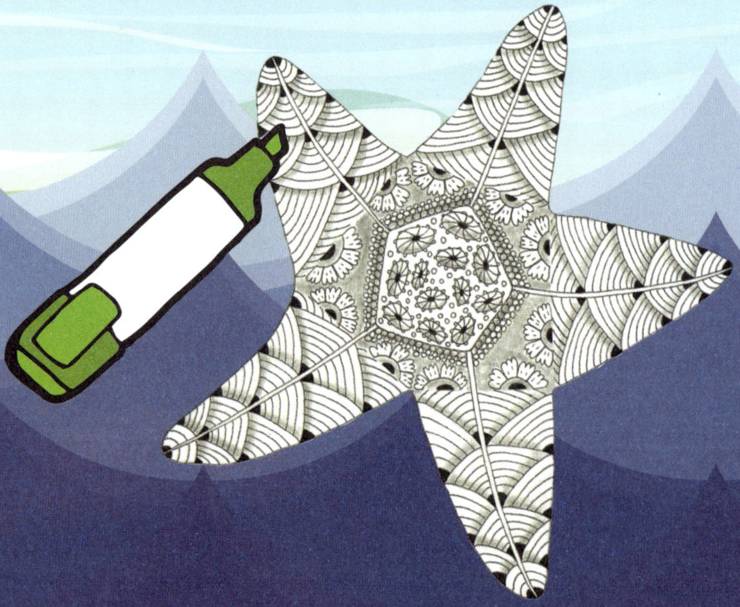

Tangling Essentials

Drawing Materials

Pencils are good for drawing "strings" (see p6) and for adding shade to your tangles. A 01 (0.25 mm) black pen is good for fine lines. Use a 05 (0.45 mm) or 08 (0.50 mm) pen to fill in bigger areas. You can use paints to brighten up your art, too!

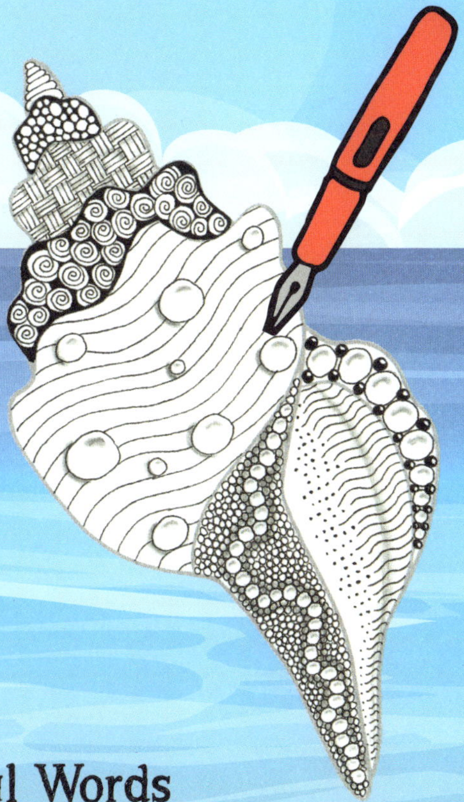

Paper

Tangles are usually drawn on a square 9 cm (3.5 inch) tile (a paper square). You can use any kind of scrap paper, but if you want to make your tangles really special use good quality art paper. Have some tracing paper on hand so you can trace images to use as outlines for your Zentangle Inspired Artworks.

Useful Words

There are some special words you might come across when you tangle. A "highlight" is a gap in the lines of your tangles. They can make your art look like it's sparkling! An "aura" is a line traced around the inside or outside of your tangle. Use auras to create a ripple effect in your pictures.

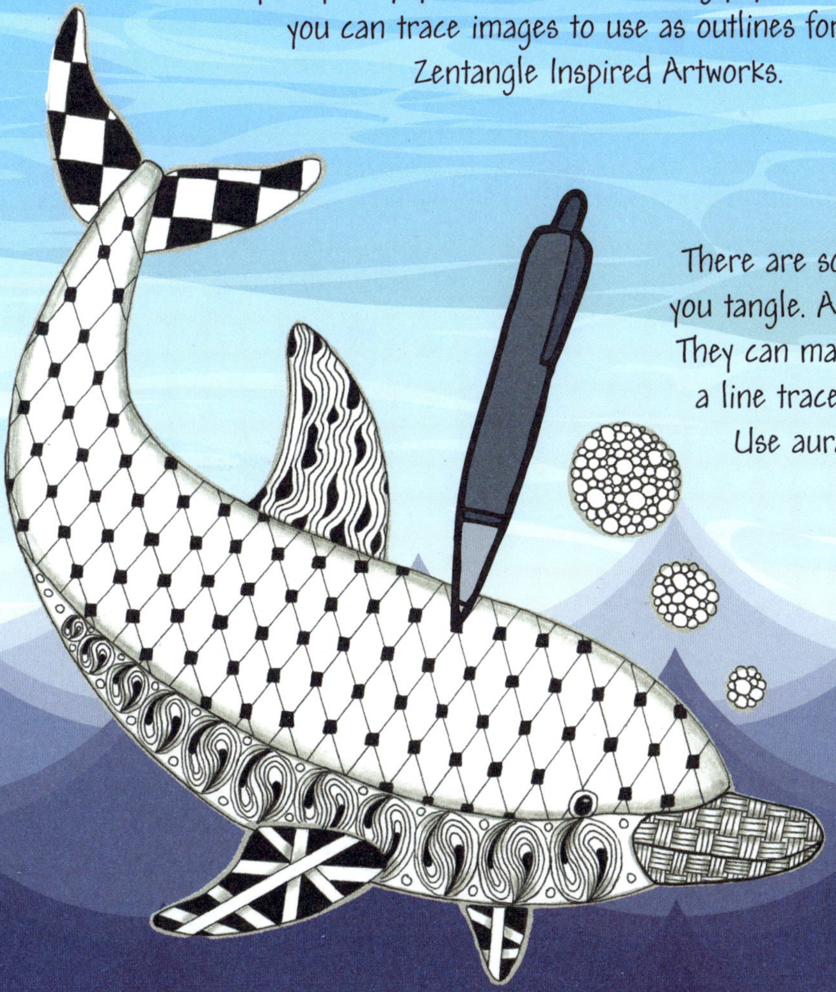

Using Strings

Strings are used to split up a large space and create smaller areas that you can tangle. They are usually drawn in pencil. I've used strings to split this square into four even triangles, but you can draw strings in any pattern you like!

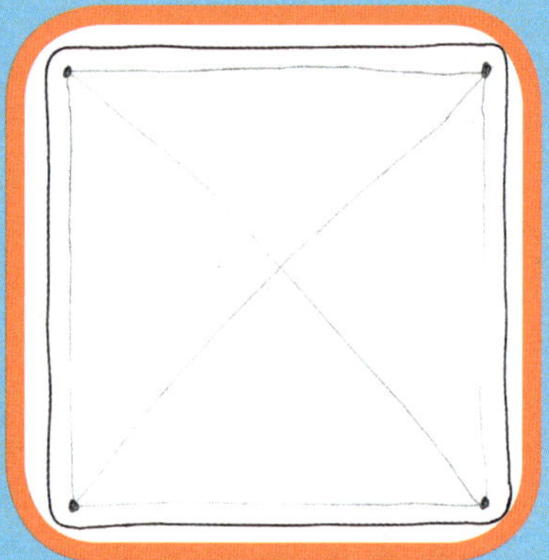

1. Use a pencil to draw a dot in each corner. Join the dots together to form a square and draw two diagonal lines across it.

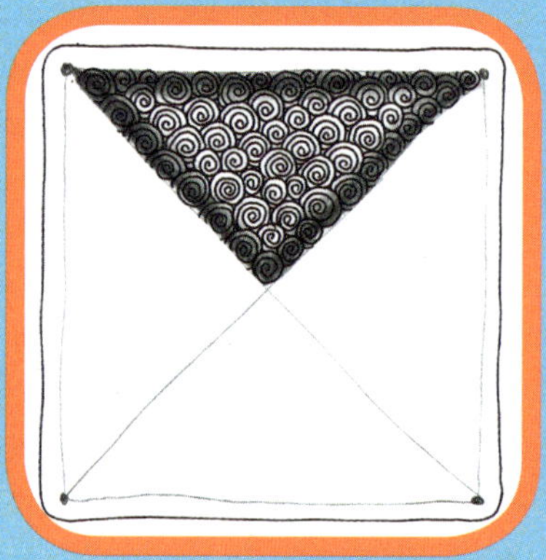

2. Fill the top triangle with Printemps (p26).

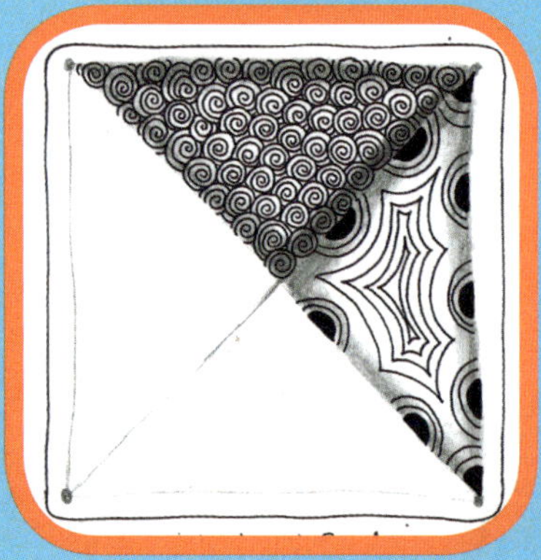

3. Then fill the right-hand triangle with Crescent Moon (p8).

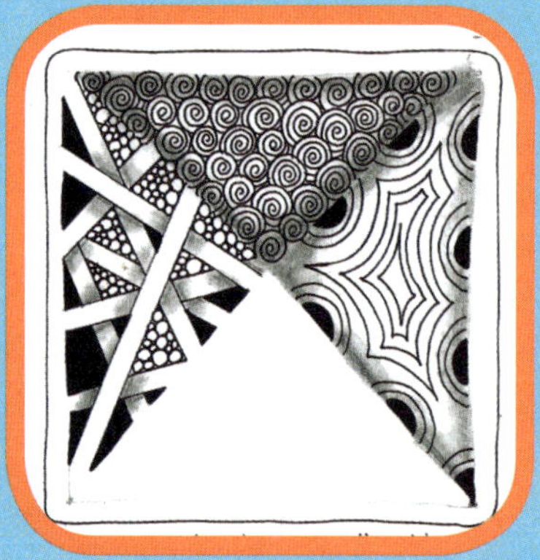

4. Fill the left-hand triangle with Hollibaugh (p31).

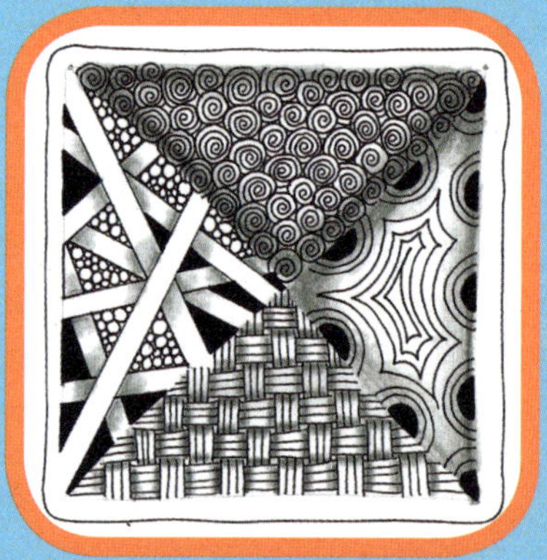

5. Finally, fill the bottom triangle with Keeko (p9).

Simple Tangles

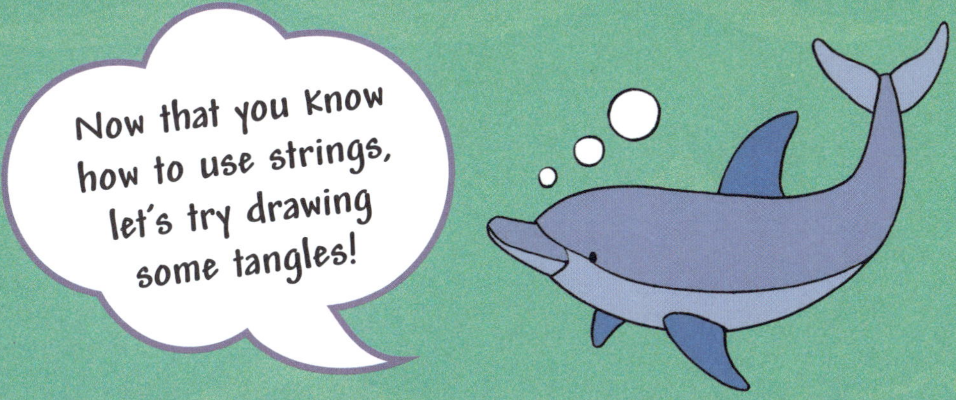

Tipple

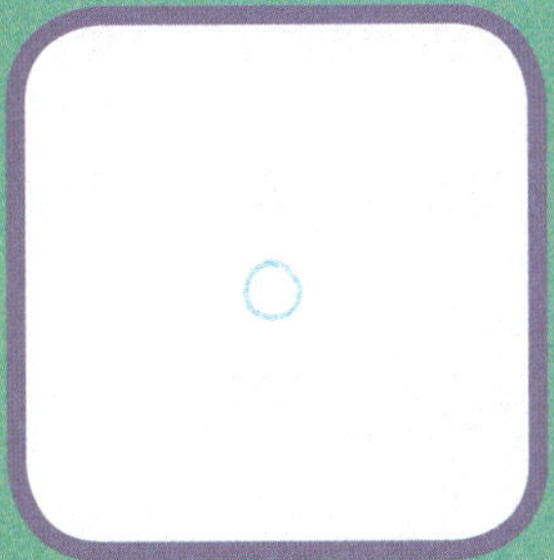

1. Start with a small circle.

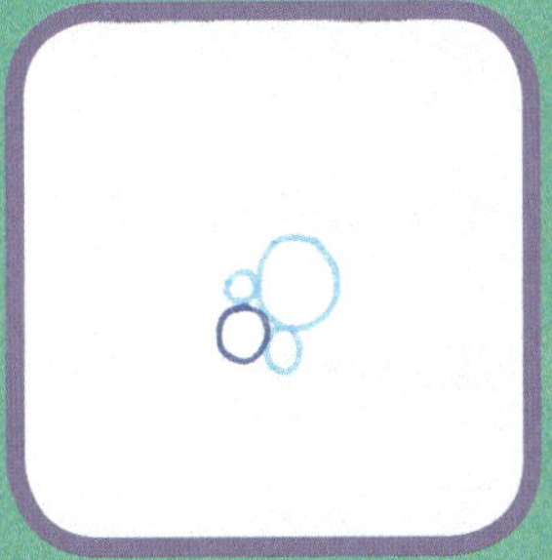

2. Add more circles of different sizes around the first circle. Each circle should touch the circle next to it.

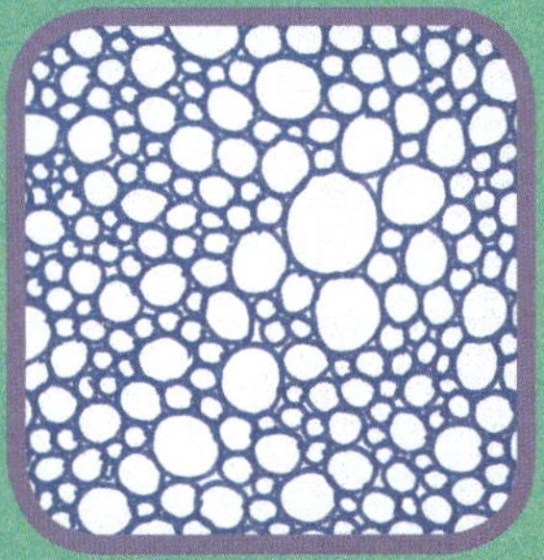

3. Continue to add more circles of different sizes until you've filled your space.

Florz

1. Draw evenly-spaced diagonal lines across your paper.

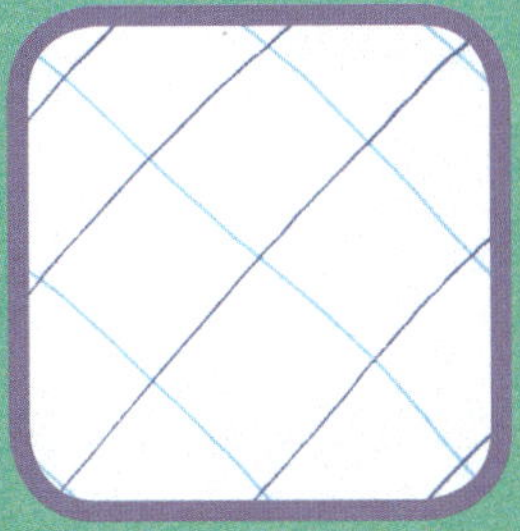

2. Draw diagonal lines going in the opposite direction.

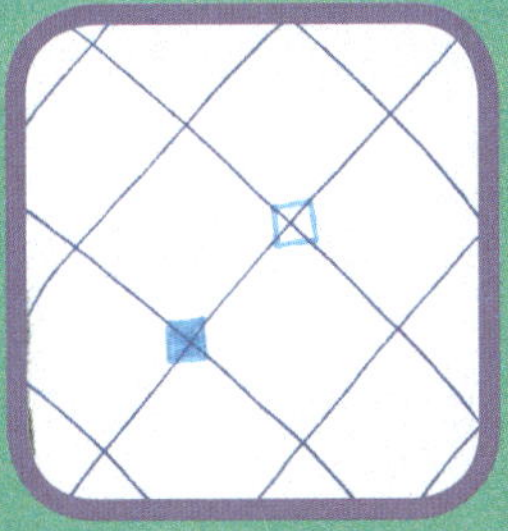

3. Add a small square in each spot where the two lines meet.

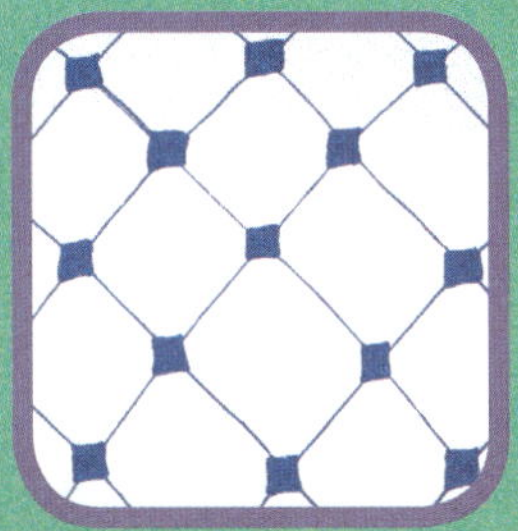

4. Continue adding more squares to finish your tangle.

Nipa

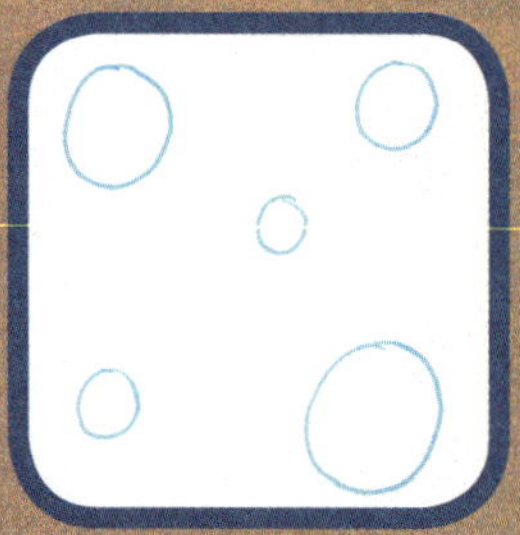

1. Start by drawing lots of different sized circles.

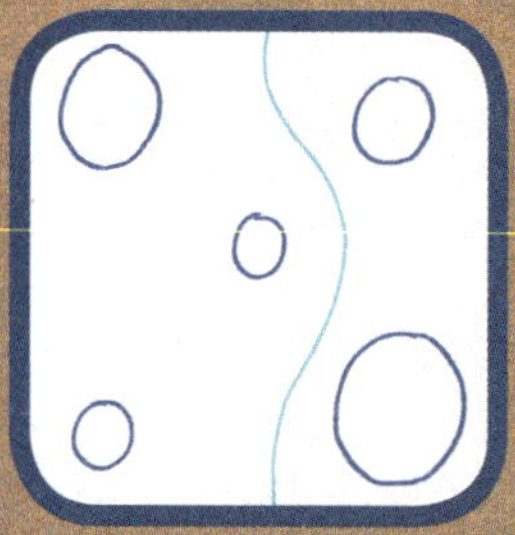

2. Draw a wobbly line from the top of the paper to the bottom.

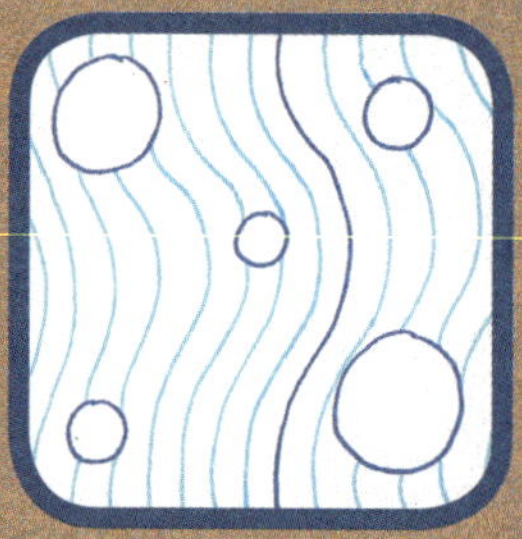

3. Draw more wobbly lines at equal distances apart, but don't draw through the circles.

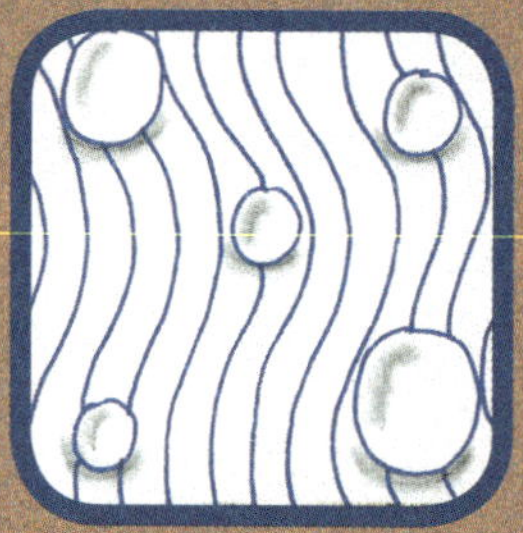

4. Use a pencil to add some smudges to your circles for extra depth.

Crescent Moon

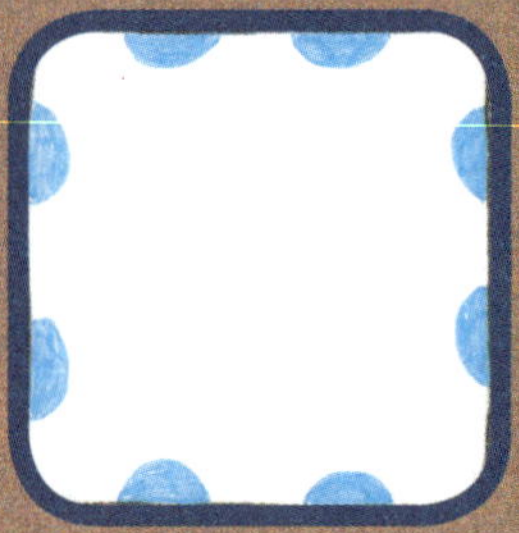

1. Start by drawing small semicircles around the edge and shade them in.

2. Draw two curved lines, called "auras", over the top of each semicircle.

3. Draw a semicircle above each of the auras. Every line should touch the previous line.

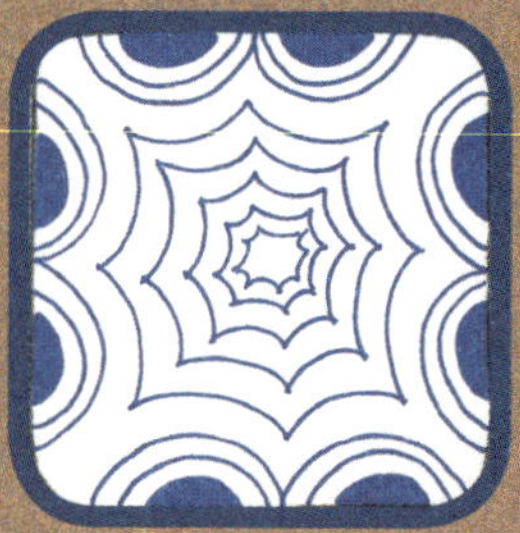

4. Repeat this pattern until the whole area is full.

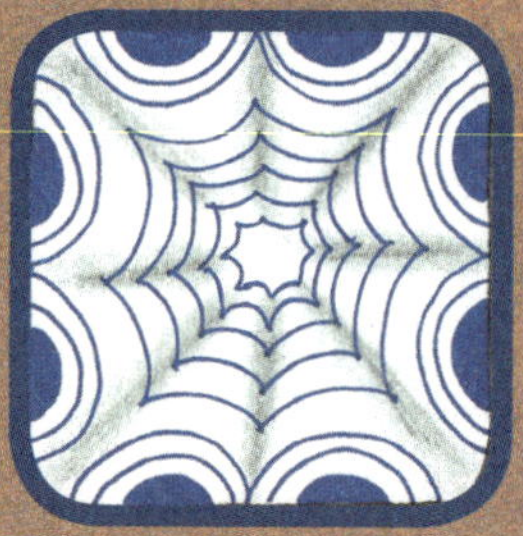

5. Draw a pencil line across the page where each of the auras meet and smudge it for a 3-D effect.

Flukes

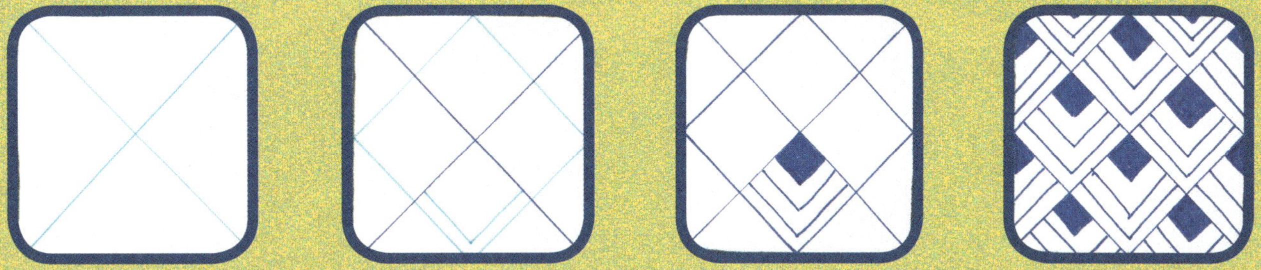

1. Draw two diagonal lines across your paper.

2. Draw a diamond shape over the lines you've just made. In the top square, add two more lines that meet at the top.

3. Draw two more lines below the first pair. Add another two lines below these to form a square and shade this in.

4. Repeat this pattern in each empty square.

Keeko

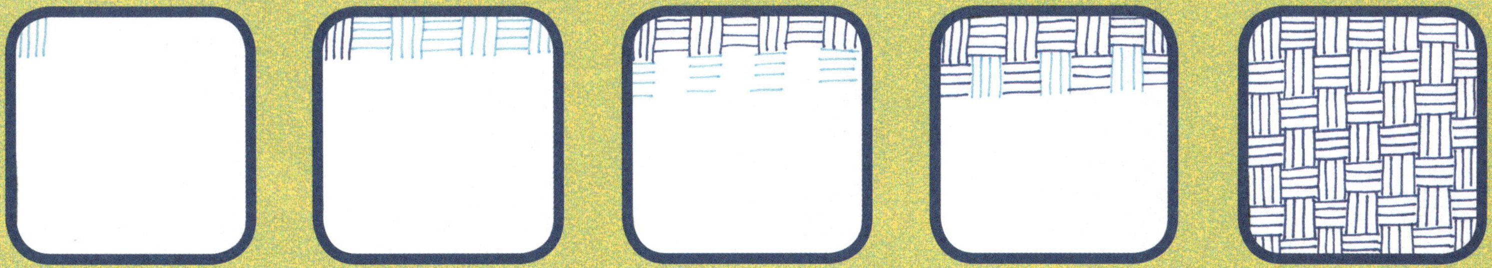

1. Start by drawing four evenly spaced vertical lines. They can be straight or slightly curved but need to stay the same throughout.

2. Draw four more lines going the opposite way (horizontally) and touching the first set. Continue this pattern of vertical and horizontal lines across the row.

3. Repeat the pattern on the second row, but this time draw the horizontal lines first, like this.

4. Then add the vertical lines.

5. Repeat until you have filled your page. Always make sure that the sets of lines go in the opposite direction to the sets on either side and above them.

Super Starfish

Follow these simple steps to create your own stunning starfish!

1. Choose your tangles and start filling in the spaces between the strings. I'm using Shattuck (p30), Festune (p46), Henna Drum (p45), and Tipple (p7).

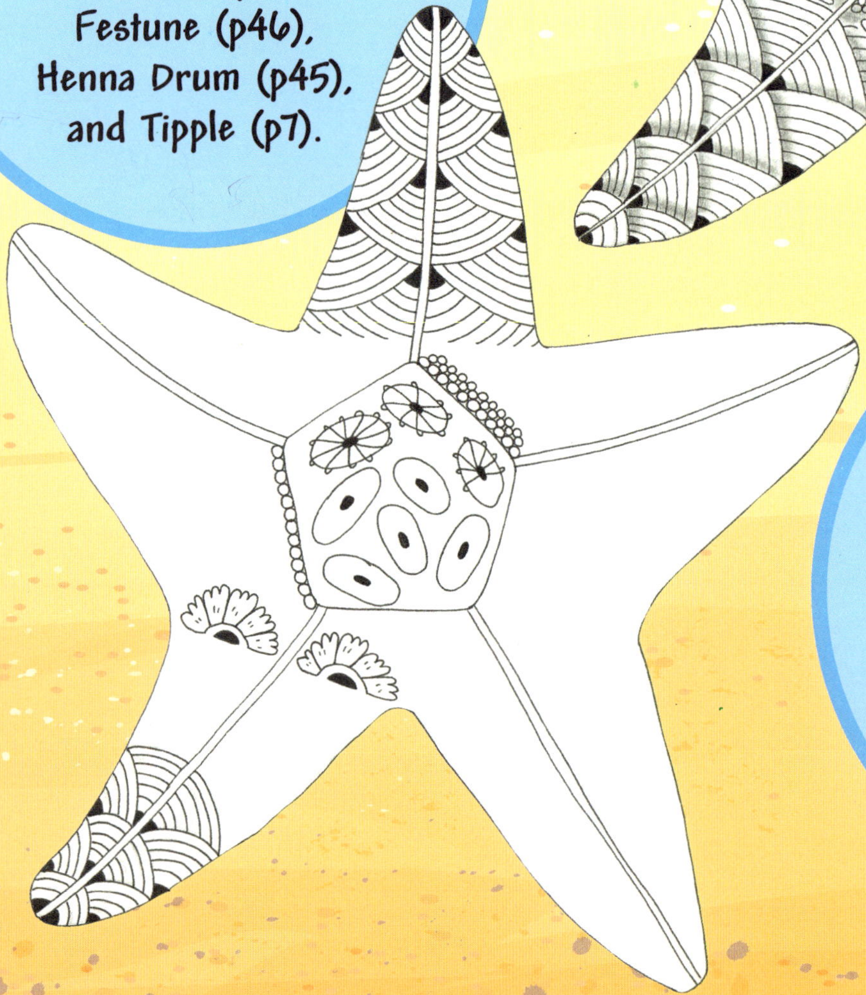

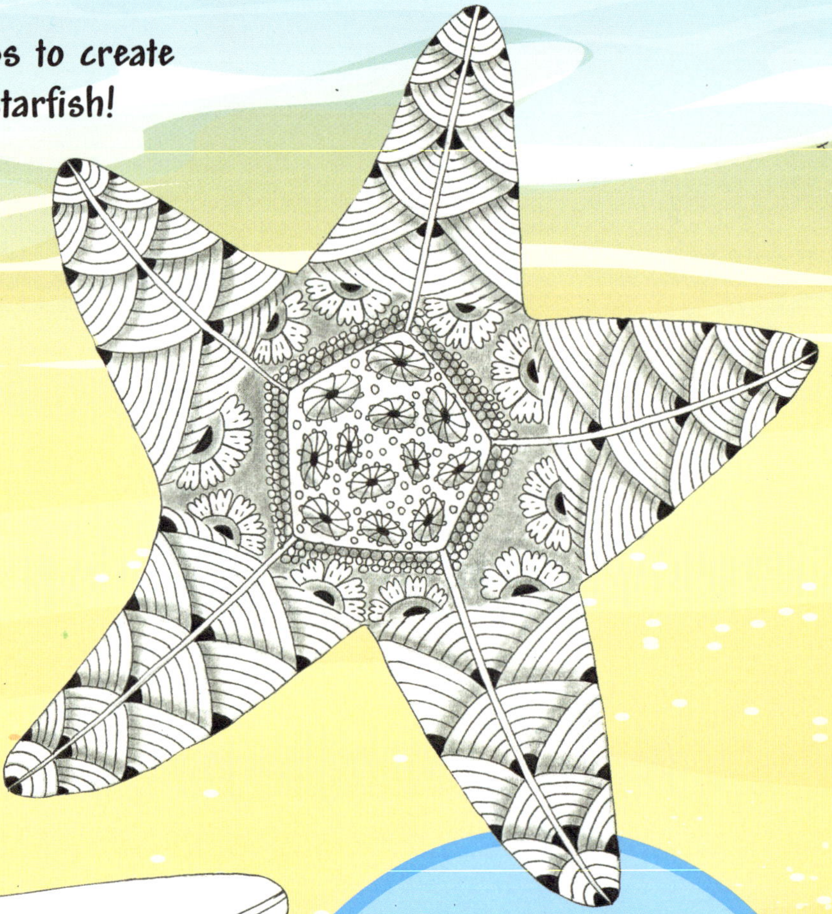

2. Continue tangling to complete your picture. I've used Shattuck to make this starfish really stand out, but you could try using a different tangle for each arm to change the look.

Tagh

Use this tangle to create some great scales on your fish pictures!

1. Start by drawing a bump in the corner of your paper.

2. Add more bumps on either side of the first one.

3. Draw a second row of bumps, beginning each line in the middle of the shape on the row below.

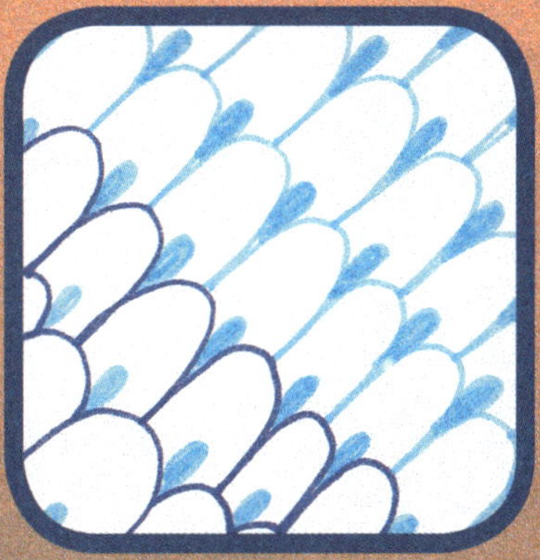

4. Continue until your paper is full. Draw an oval shape in the small gaps where each bump meets another, and fill these in with your pen to finish.

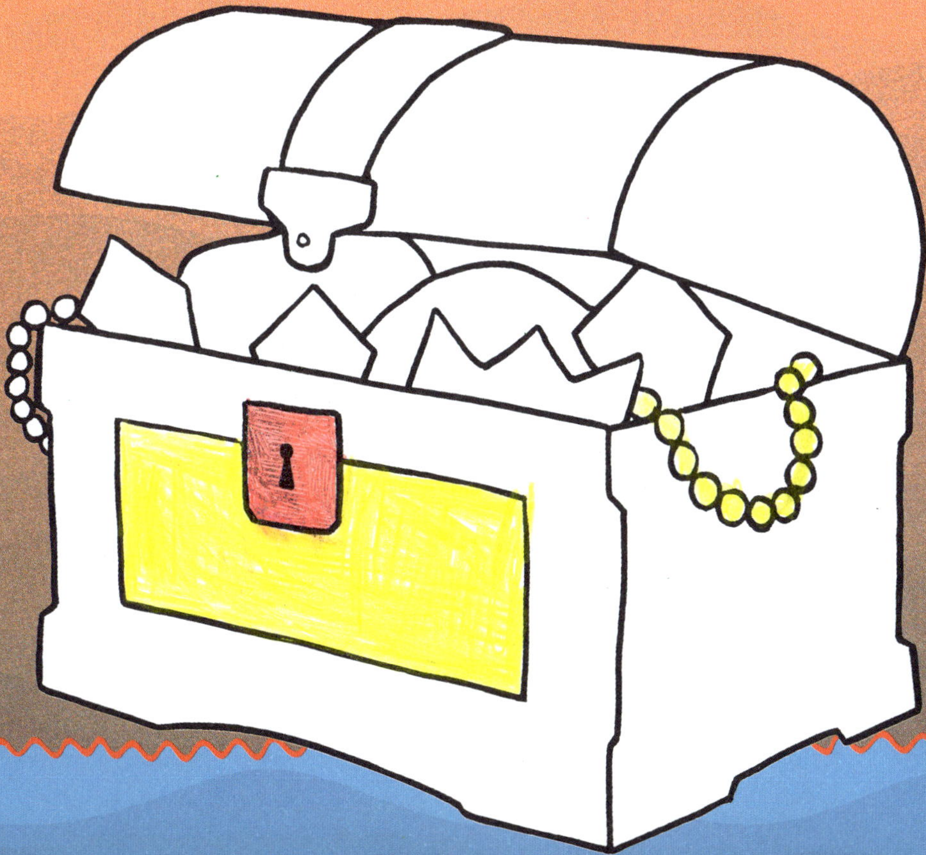

Fabulous Fish

Use some of your best tangles to fill in this beautiful fish!

2. Fill up the space using lots of tangles. I've used Shattuck (p30) for the body and Printemps (p26) for the back fins.

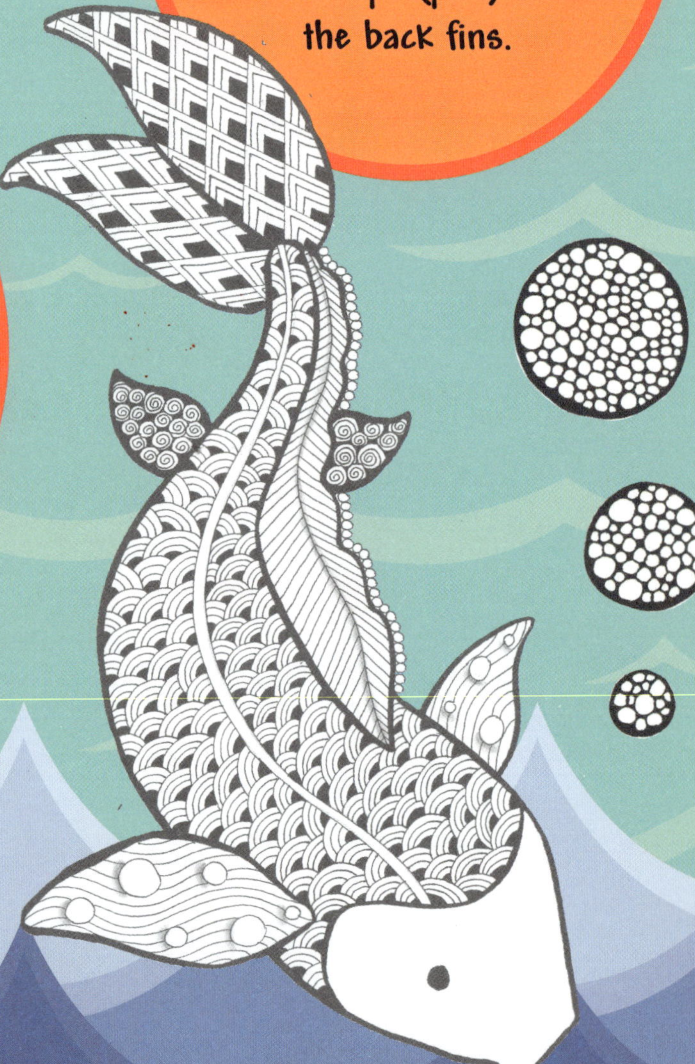

1. Start to add some tangles to the outline. I've chosen Flukes (p9) for the tail, Tipple (p7) for the bubbles, Meer (p40) for the fin on its back, and Nipa (p8) for the front fins.

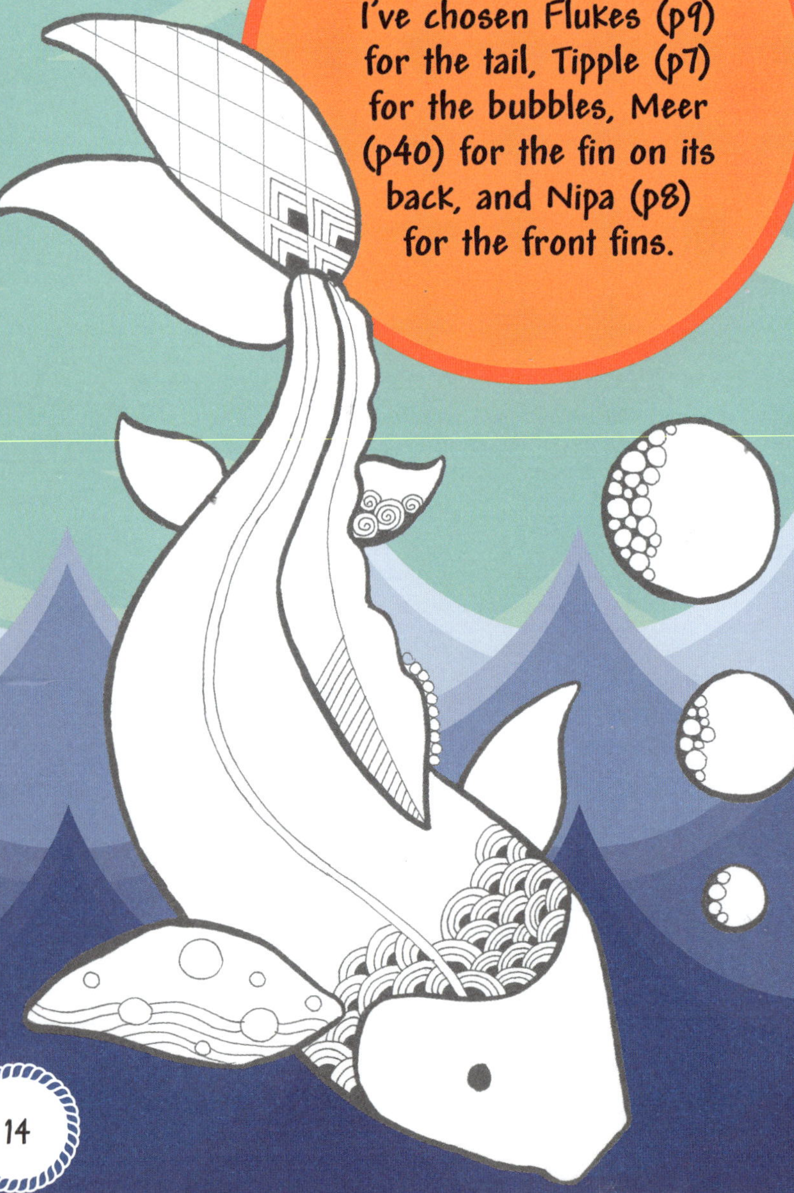

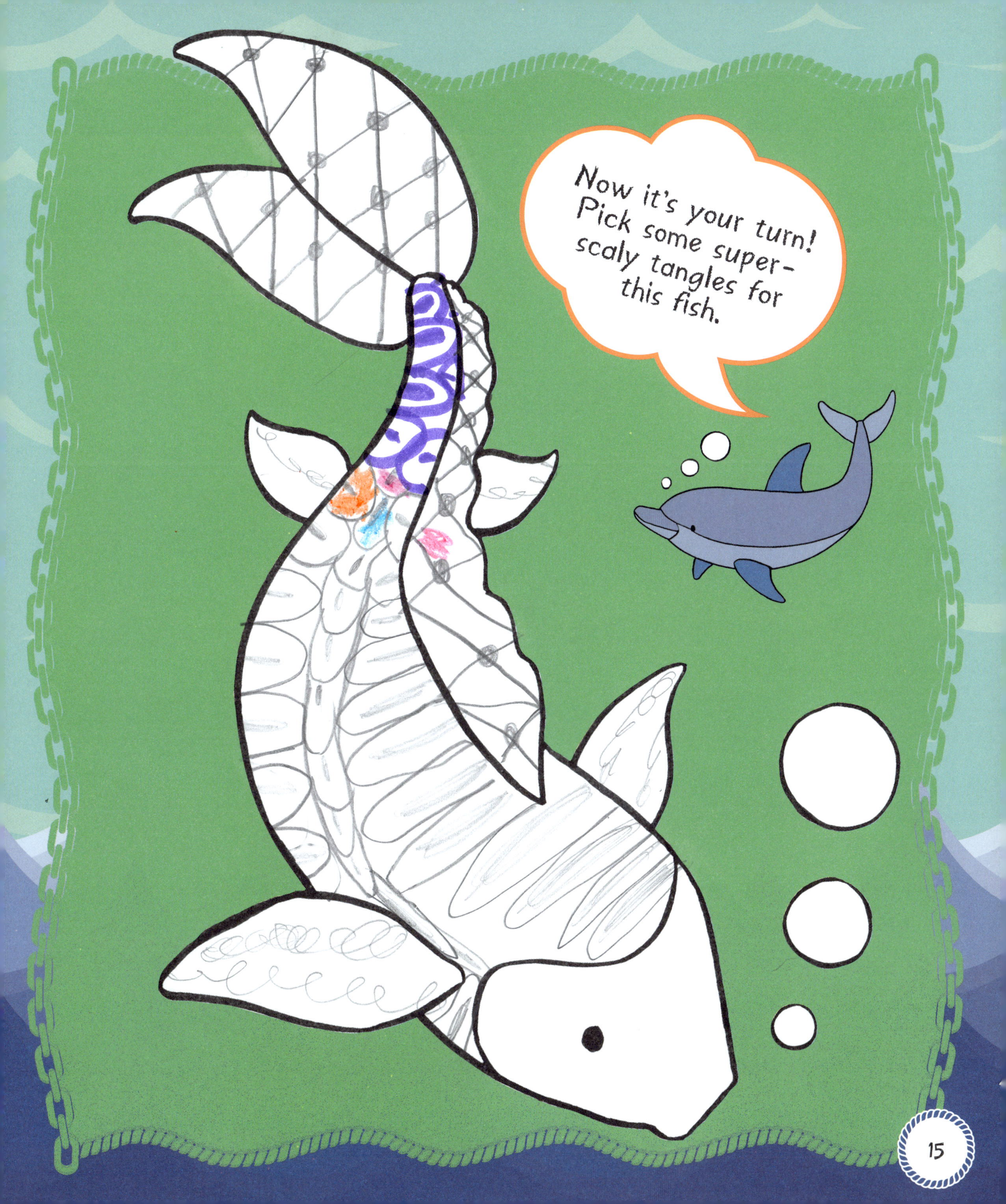
Now it's your turn! Pick some super-scaly tangles for this fish.

Tangle Time!

Use some underwater tangles to complete this coral reef picture!

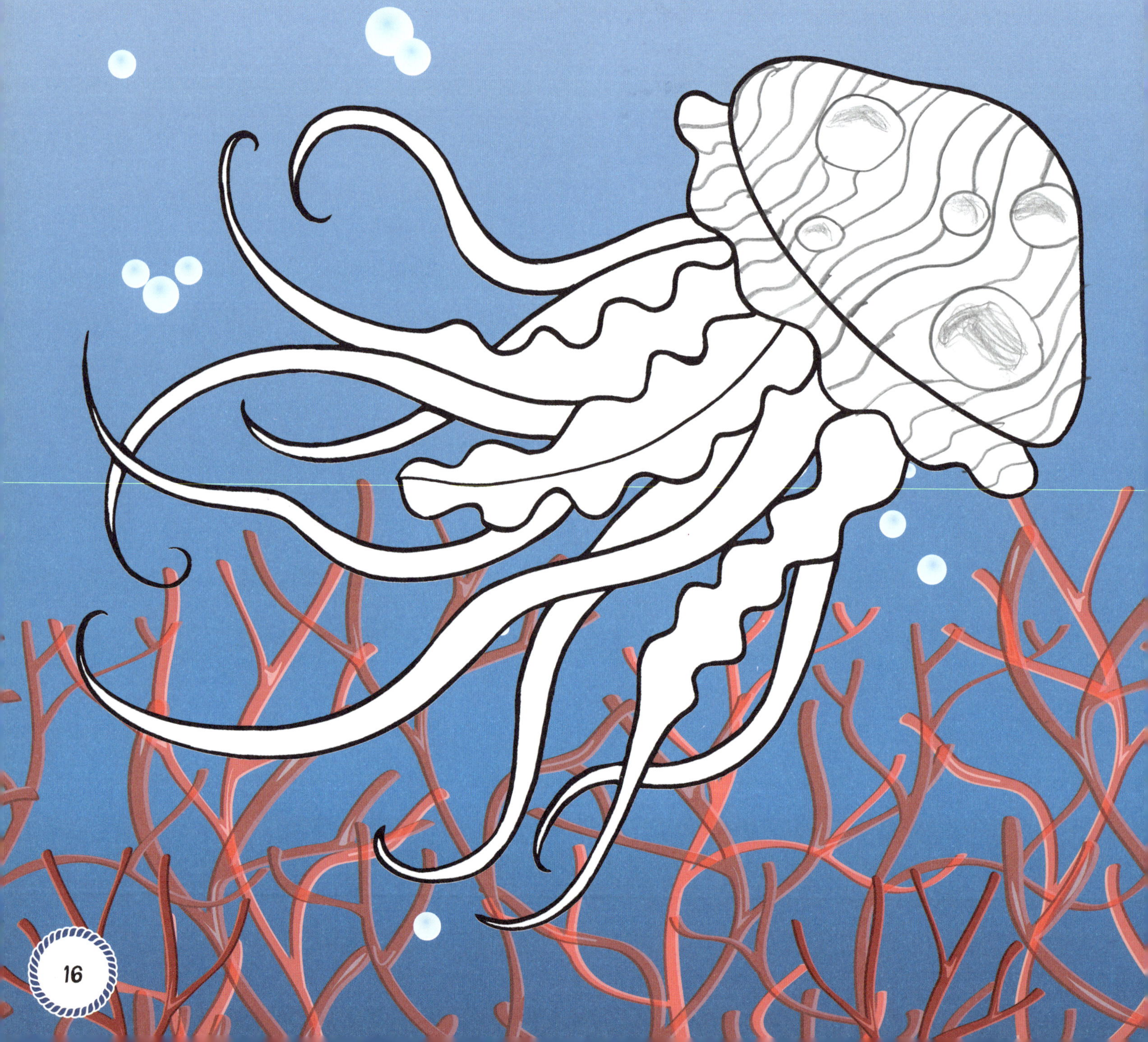

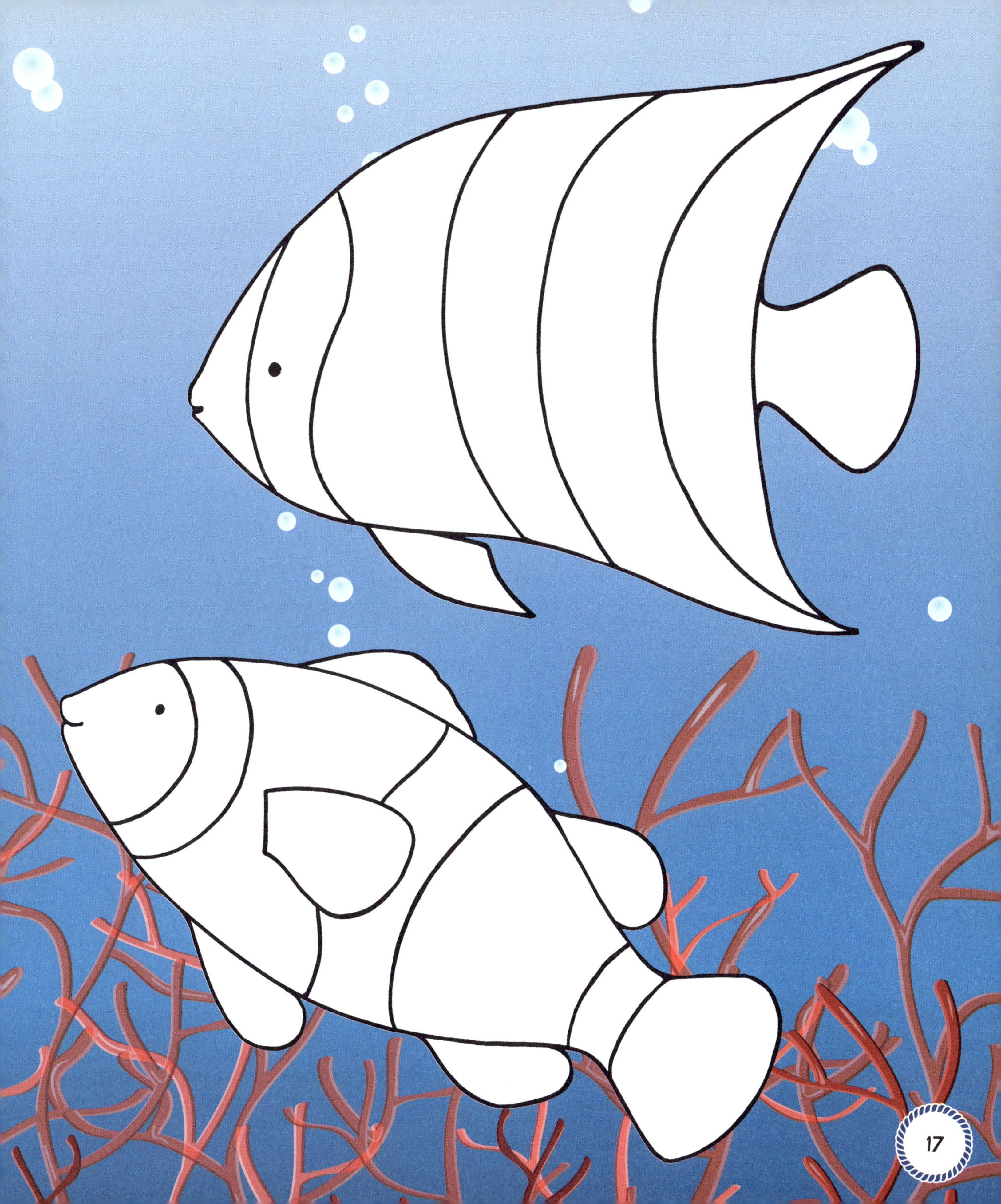

Knightsbridge

This bold tangle is a great way to make your sea creatures stand out.

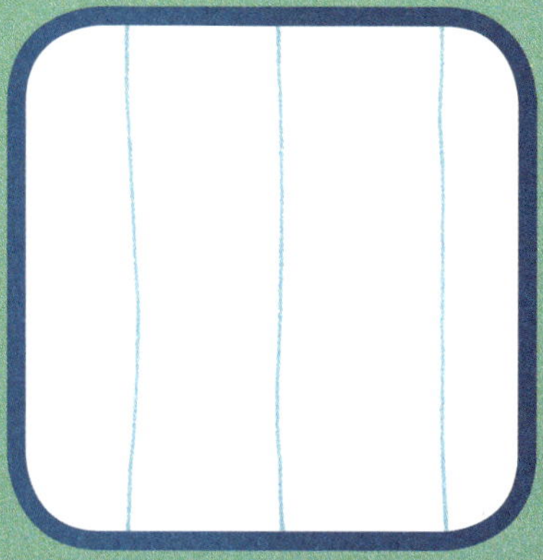

1. Start by drawing evenly-spaced vertical lines across your paper.

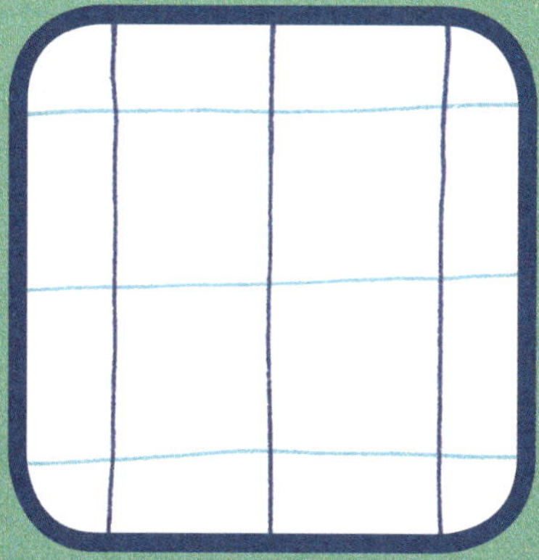

2. Now add some horizontal lines to create a grid.

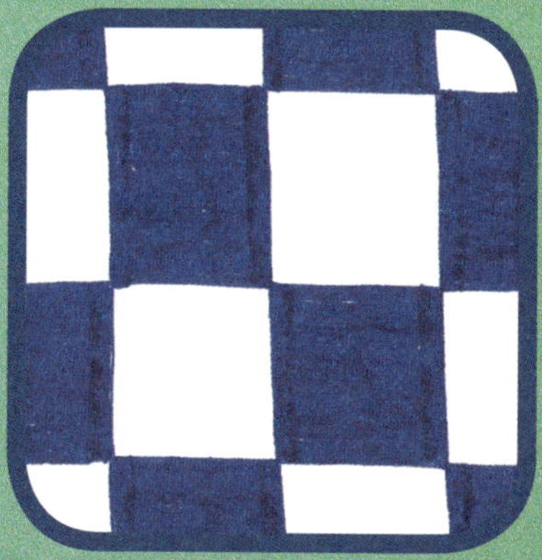

3. Use your pen to fill in each alternate square to create a pattern like this.

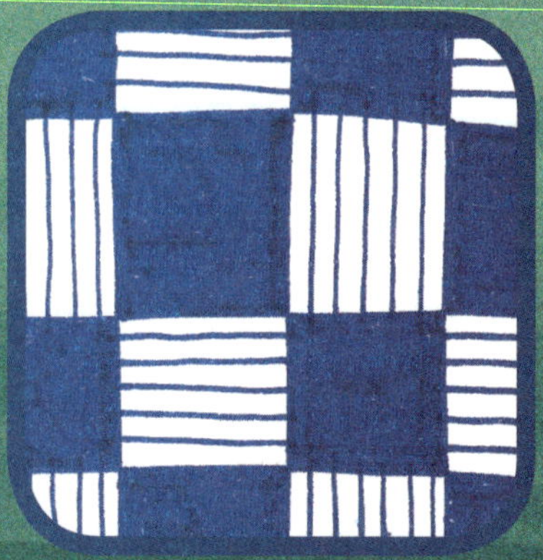

4. You can add patterns in the empty squares too, if you like.

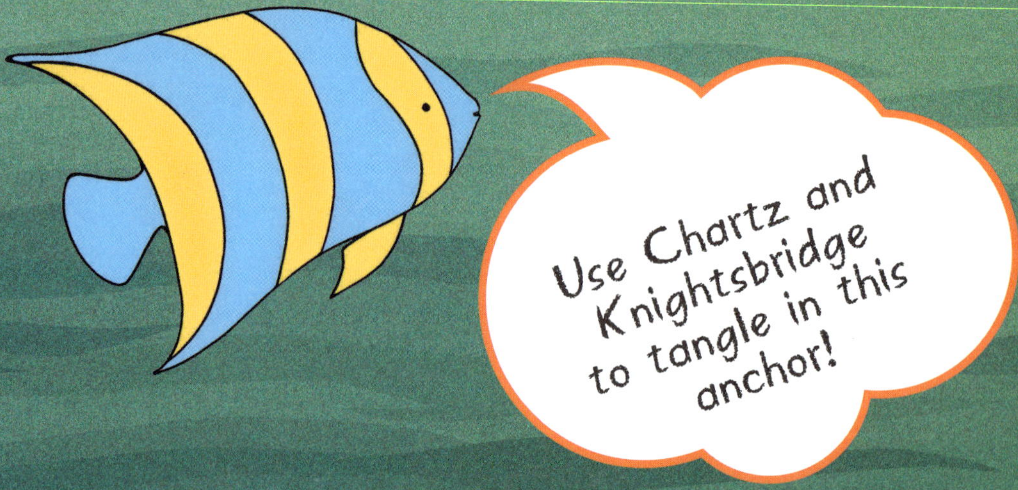

Chartz

The zigzags in this tangle give it a bit of bite. It would be ideal for a shark picture!

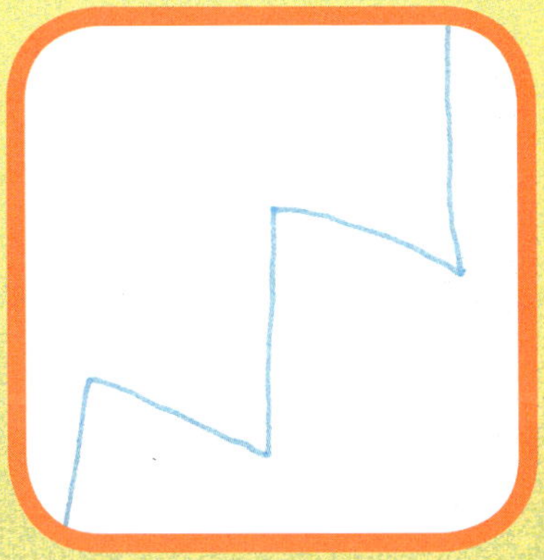

1. Start by drawing a zigzagged line across the page.

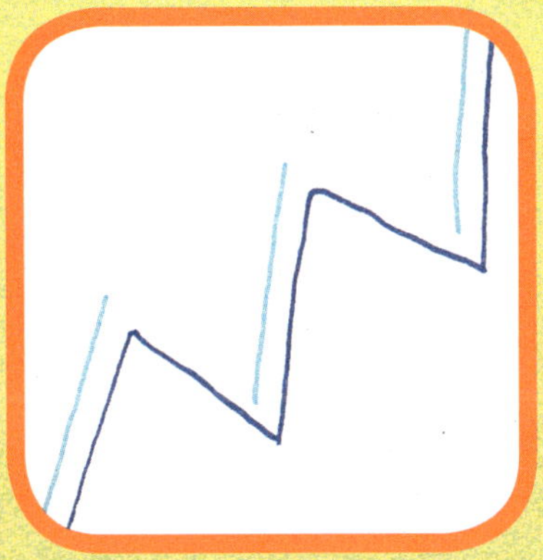

2. Draw matching lines going upward just above the first zigzag.

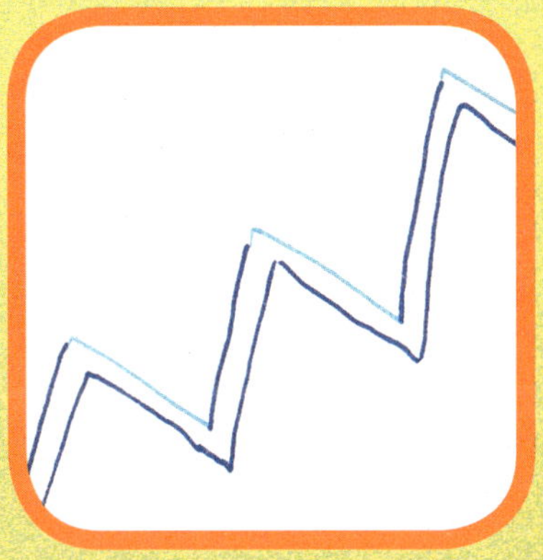

3. Then join them up by drawing matching lines going downward.

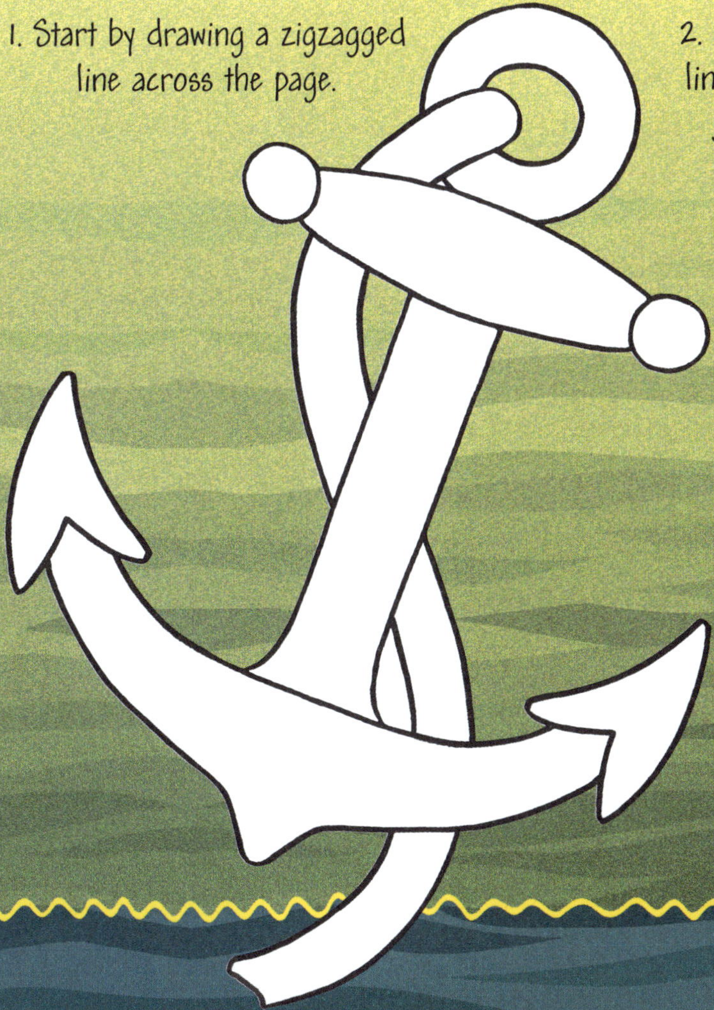

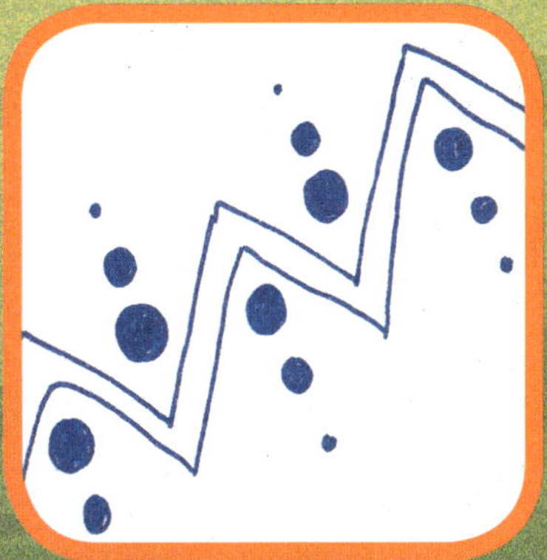

4. To finish, draw three circles in the deepest points of the zigzags. Use your pen to fill them in.

Tangled Turtle

Have fun using lots of different tangles to give your turtle a spectacular shell!

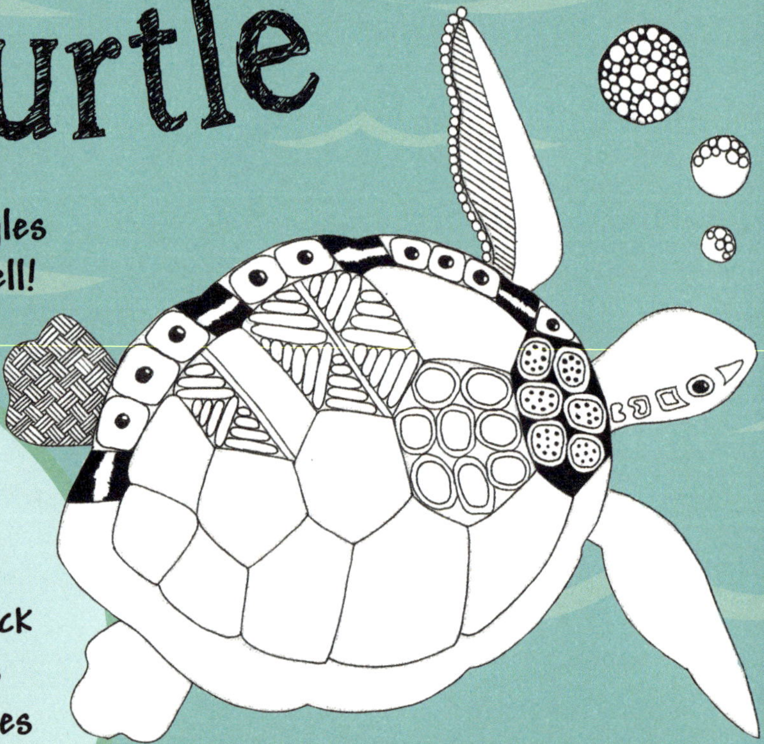

1. Start to add a few tangles to the outline. I'm going to use Shattuck (p30) and Lotus Pods (p36) as the main tangles on the shell.

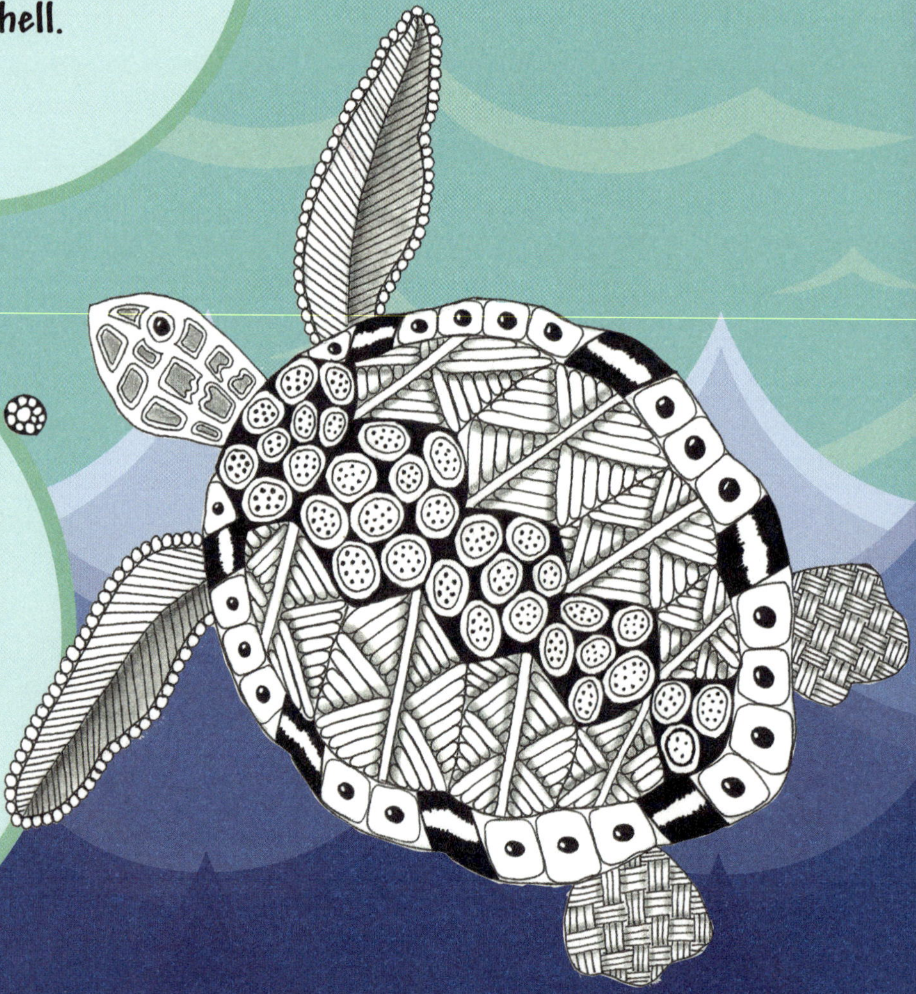

2. Continue tangling to complete your picture. I've used Meer (p40) for the front flippers and Keeko (p9) for the back feet. Filling the bubbles with Tipple (p7) adds a nice extra detail.

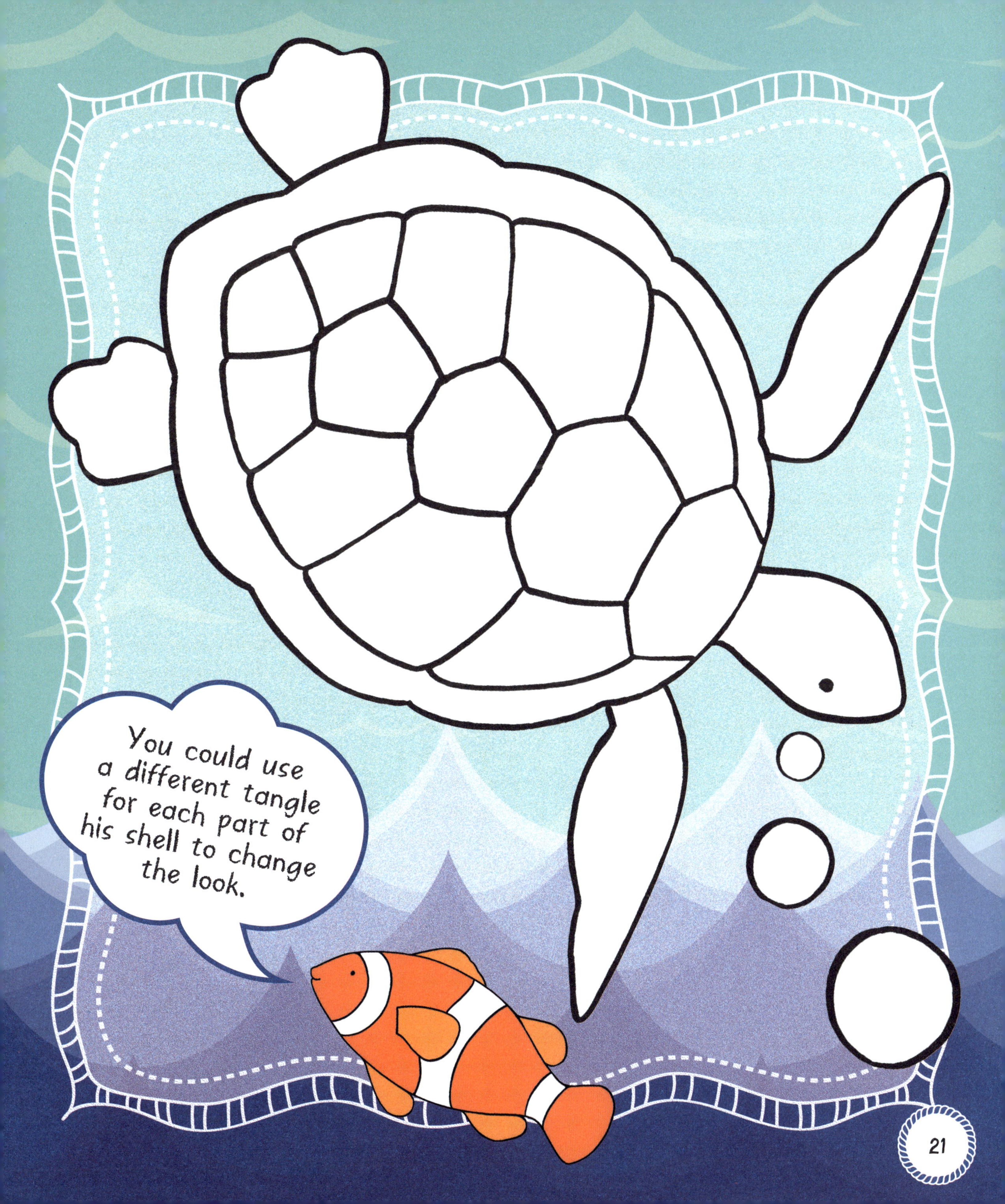
You could use a different tangle for each part of his shell to change the look.

Cruffle

A cluster of Cruffle balls would make a lovely texture for a coral reef!

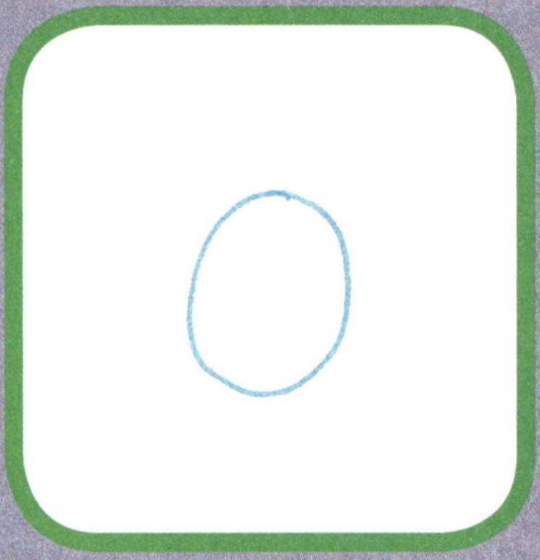

1. Start by drawing a circle.

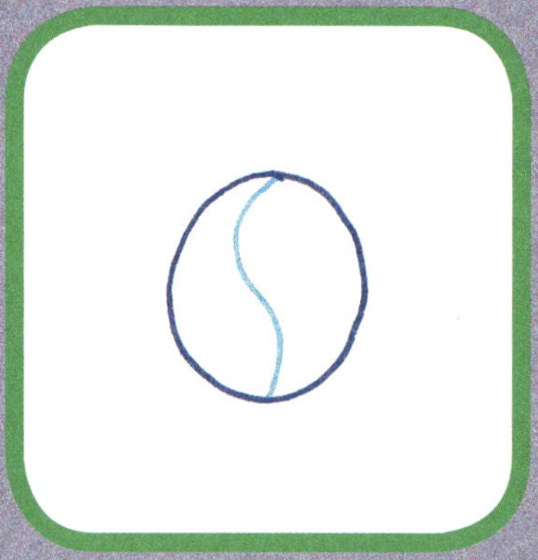

2. Draw a curved line through the middle.

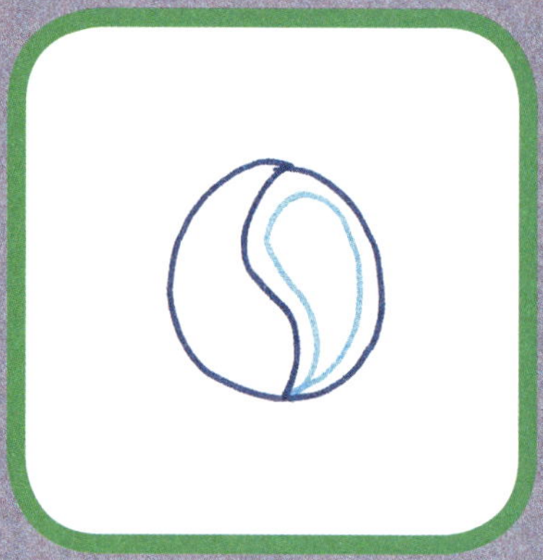

3. Draw a teardrop shape in the right-hand side of the circle.

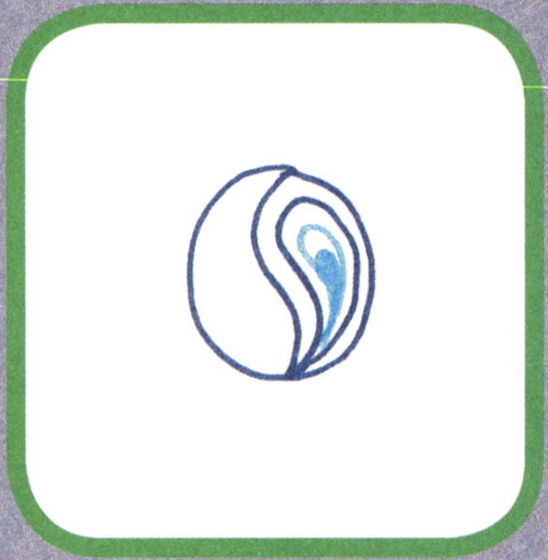

4. Draw another teardrop shape inside the one you just made and partly fill it in with your pen.

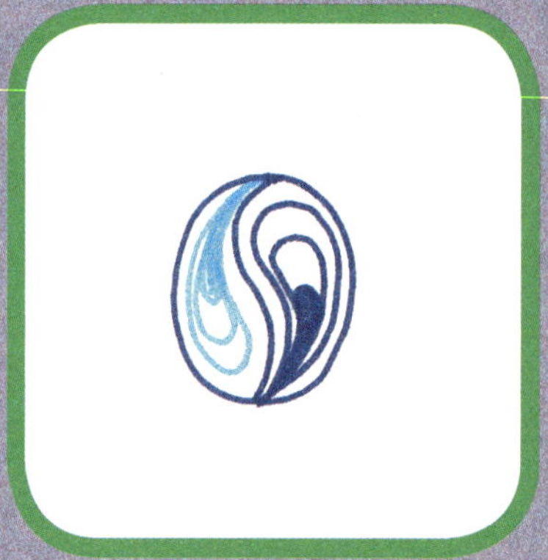

5. You can repeat steps 3-4 on the other side of the curved line, but draw the pattern upside down.

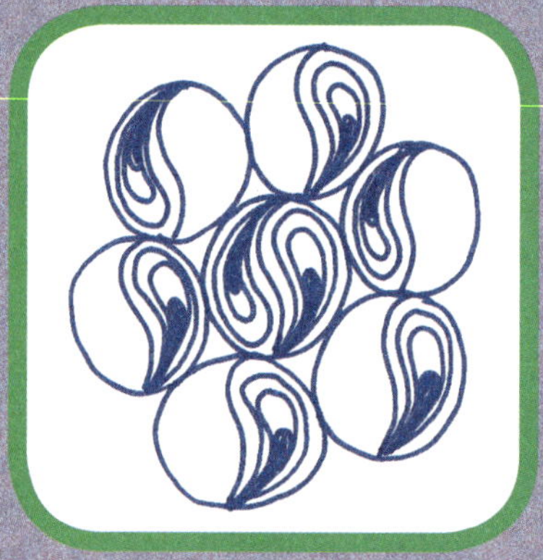

6. Add more Cruffle balls to fill up the space, if you like.

Knase

This fun tangle would make a great outline for a shark or whale picture.

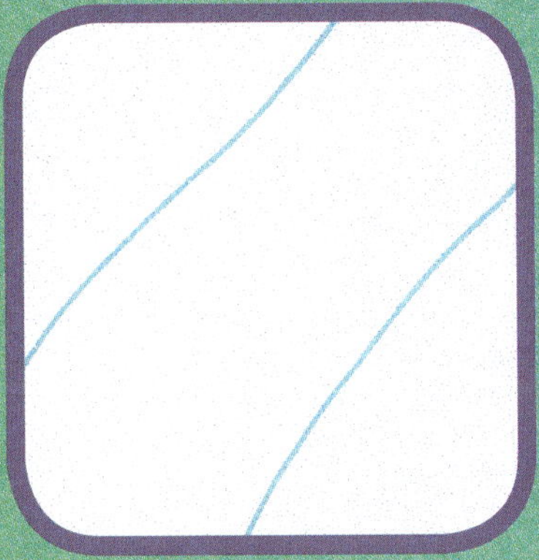

1. Start by drawing two parallel lines going from one side of the page to the other.

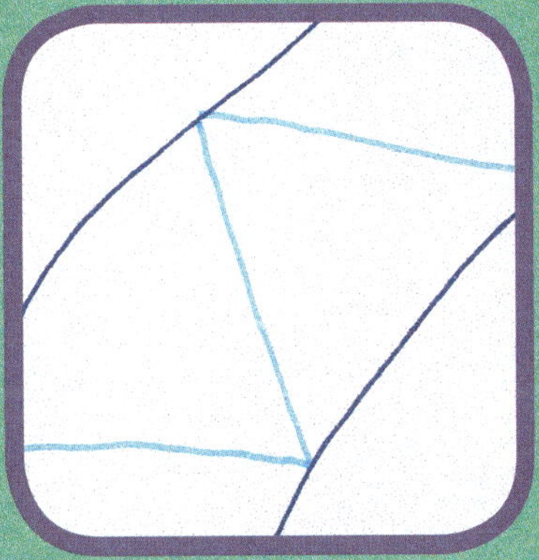

2. Draw a zigzag line in the gap between the first two lines.

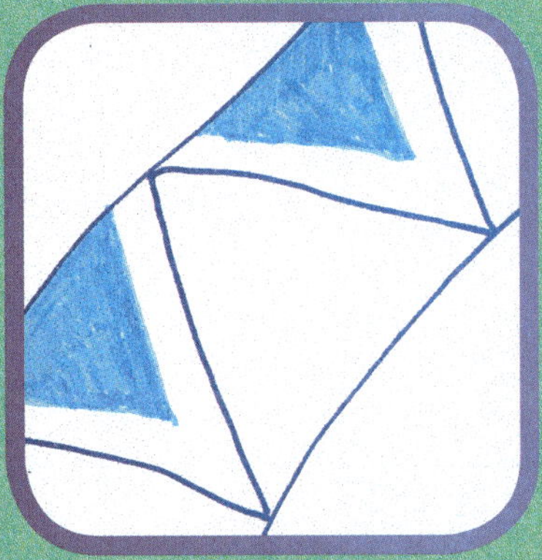

3. Draw "V" shapes inside the triangles in the top row, and shade these in.

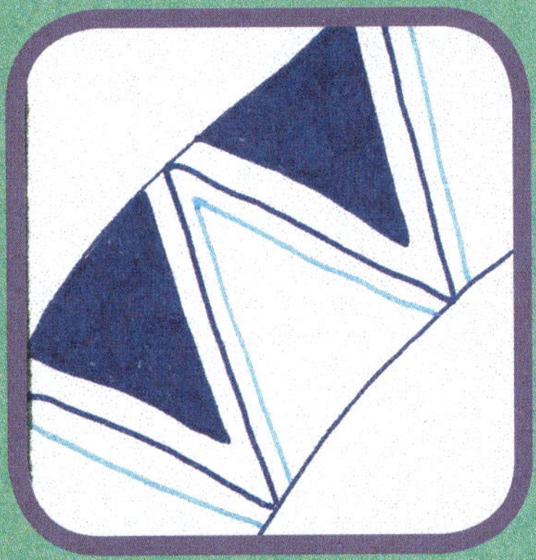

4. Draw an aura around the zigzag line in the bottom row.

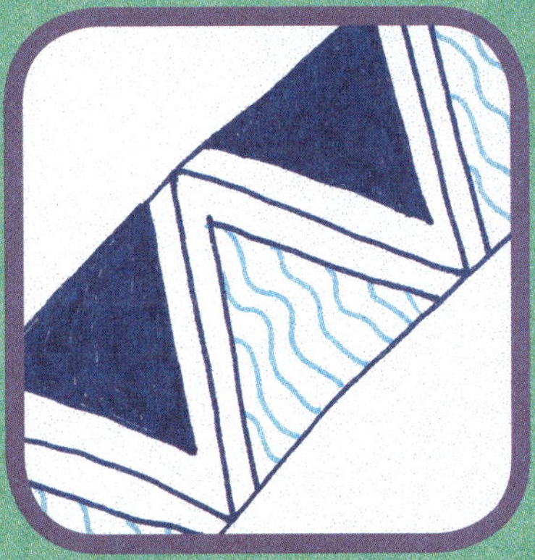

5. Now fill each triangle in the bottom row with wiggly lines to finish your tangle.

Playful Dolphin

Follow these easy steps to create your own friendly dolphin!

1. Start to fill in the spaces between the strings. I've chosen Diva Dance (p27) for the fin and Hollibaugh (p31) for the flippers.

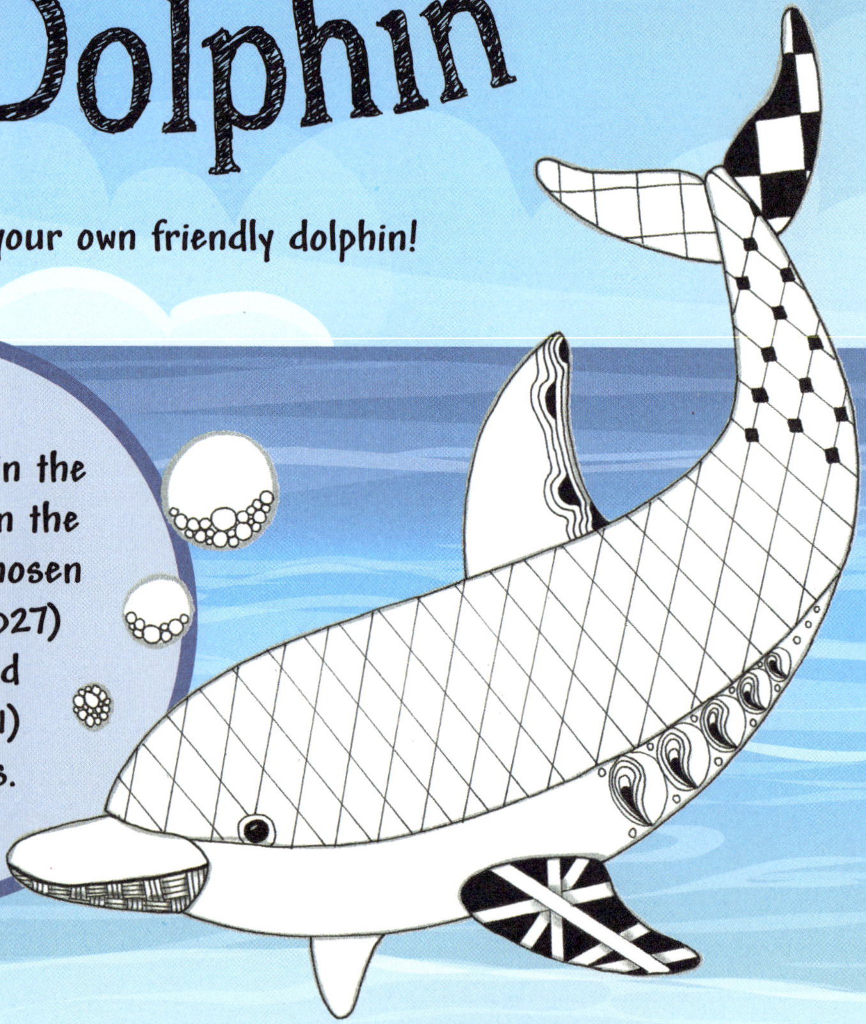

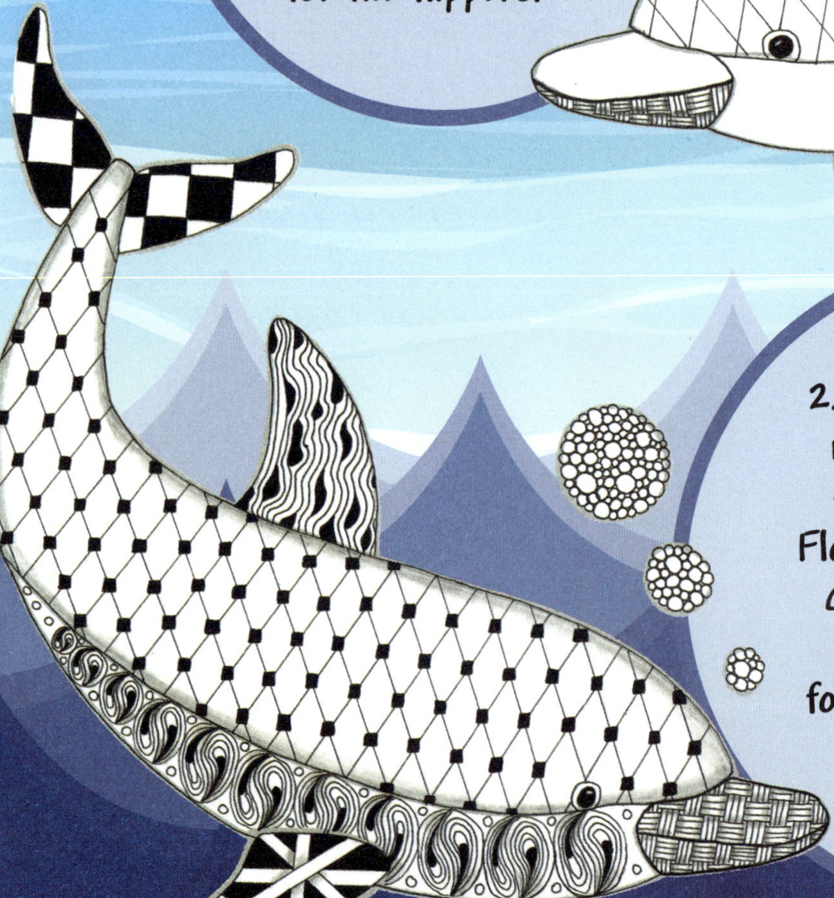

2. Knightsbridge (p18) makes the tail really stand out. I've used Florz (p7) for the body, Cruffle (p22) on the tummy, Keeko (p9) for his nose, and filled the bubbles with Tipple (p7).

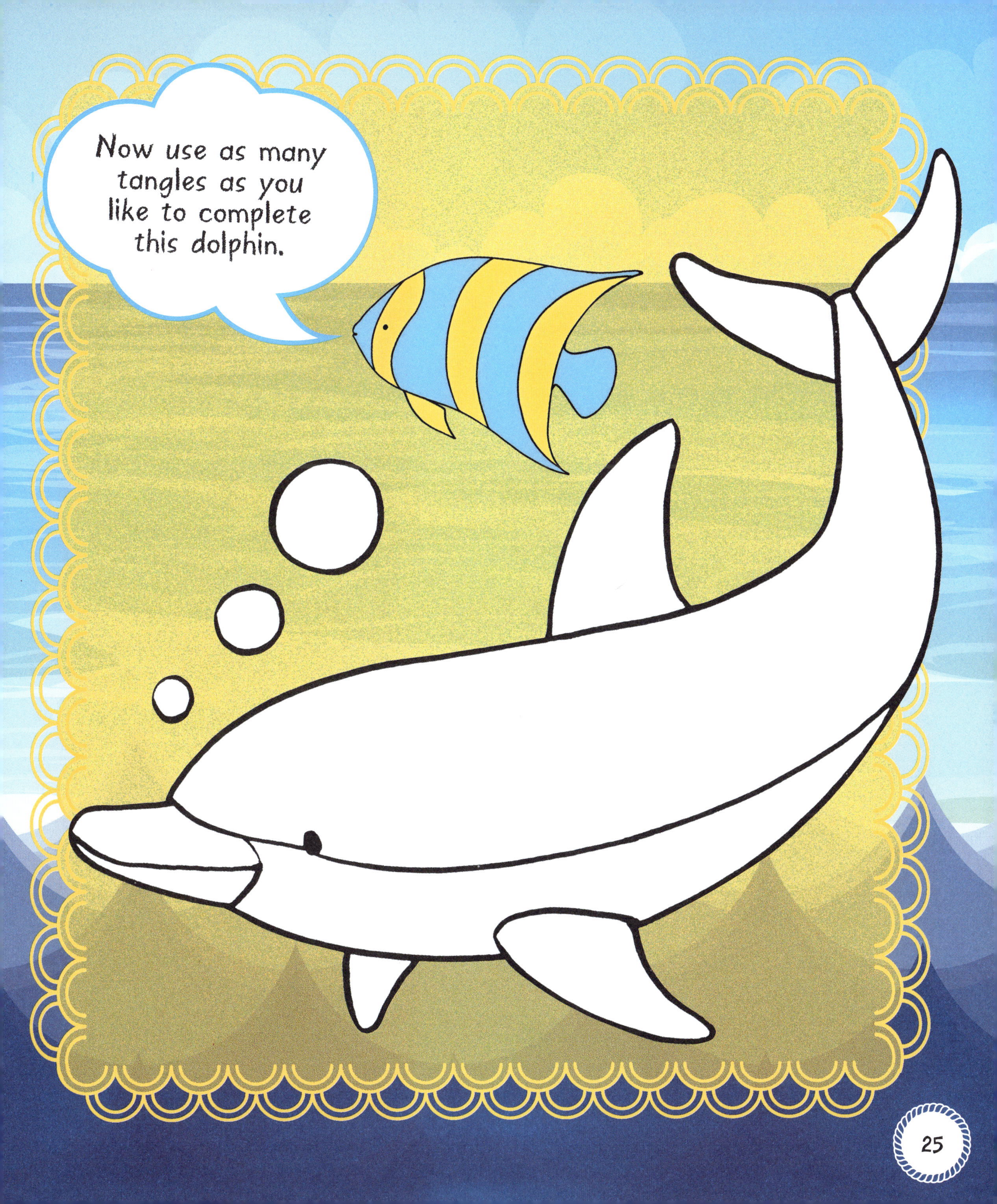
Now use as many tangles as you like to complete this dolphin.

Printemps

This tangle creates a pretty, swirly texture. It would look great on a seashell!

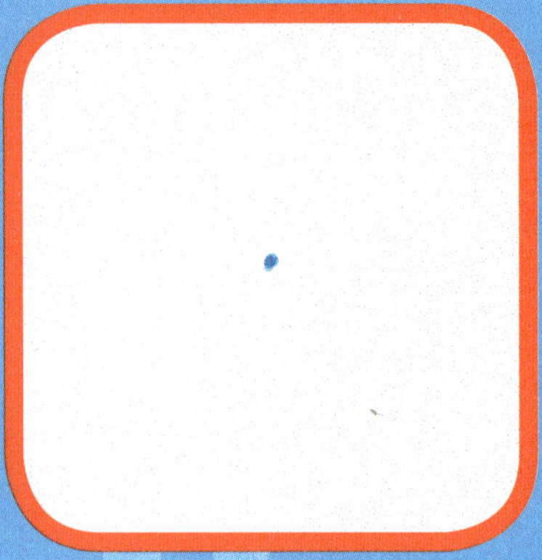

1. Start with a small dot in the middle of your paper.

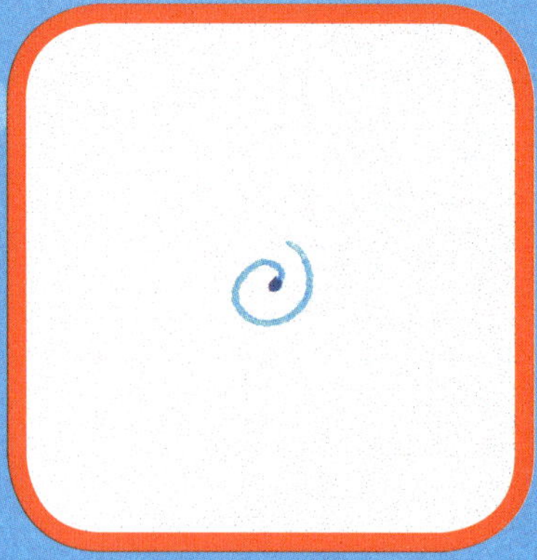

2. Draw a little swirl from the dot, using a continuous line. Keep the lines an equal distance apart.

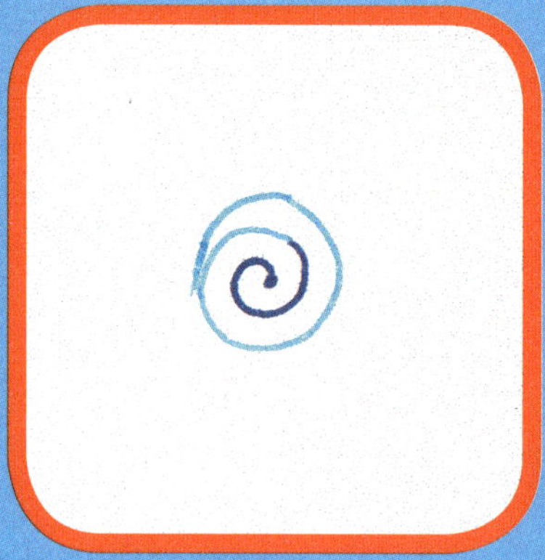

3. Continue the line around the outside of the swirl. Draw a full circle to finish.

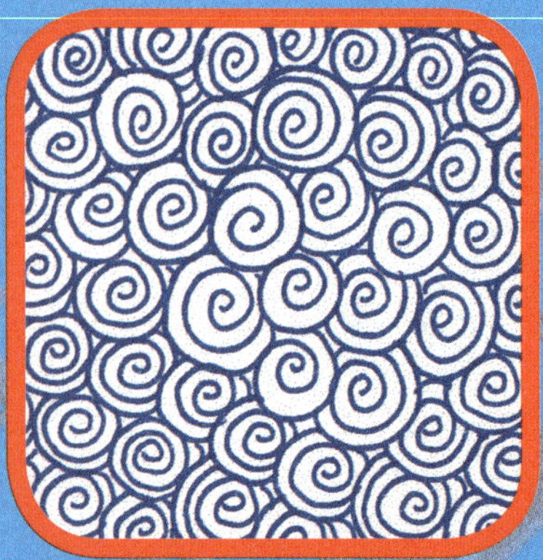

4. Repeat this swirly pattern, until you've filled the paper. Try varying the size of your swirls as you go.

5. To add a bit of sparkle to Printemps, leave a small gap (a "highlight") in the circle at step 3, like this.

Try using Printemps and Diva Dance on me!

Diva Dance

Diva Dance looks a lot like seaweed swaying in the sea. It'll add a sense of movement to any picture!

1. Draw two slightly wobbly lines, evenly spaced apart, down the left-hand side.

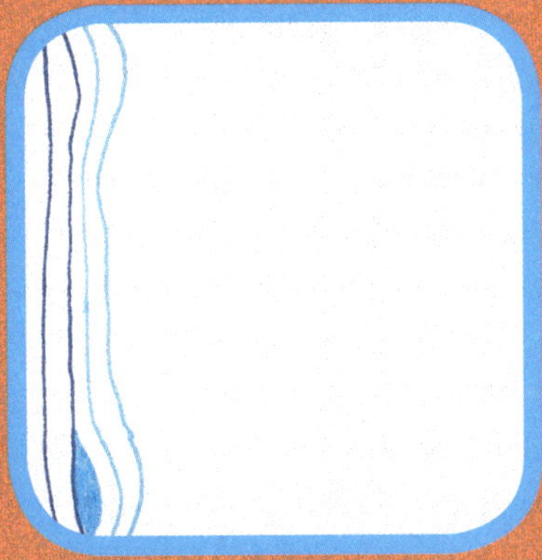

2. Add a small bump to the second line and fill it in. Then draw a second pair of lines that flow around the bump.

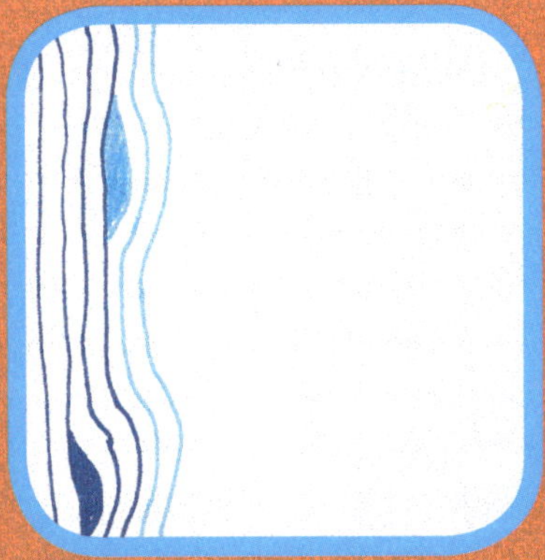

3. Add another bump on a different part of the last line. Draw two lines around it.

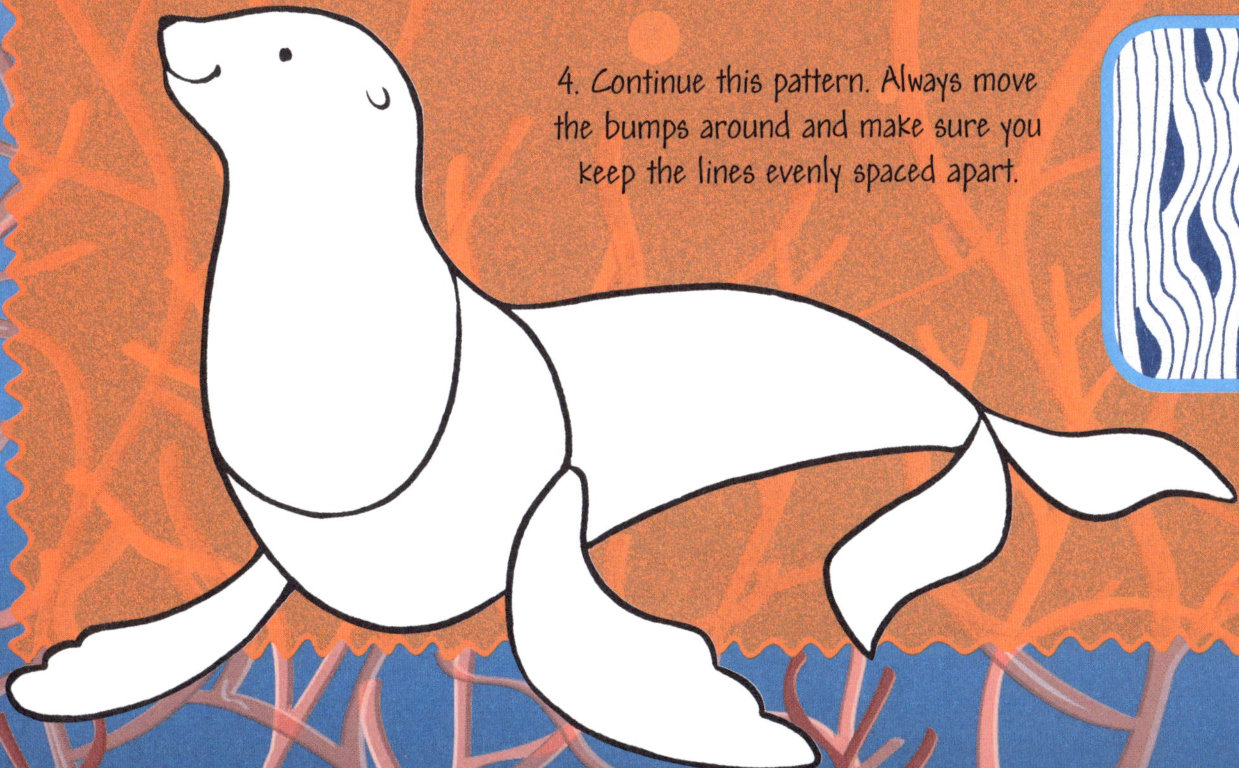

4. Continue this pattern. Always move the bumps around and make sure you keep the lines evenly spaced apart.

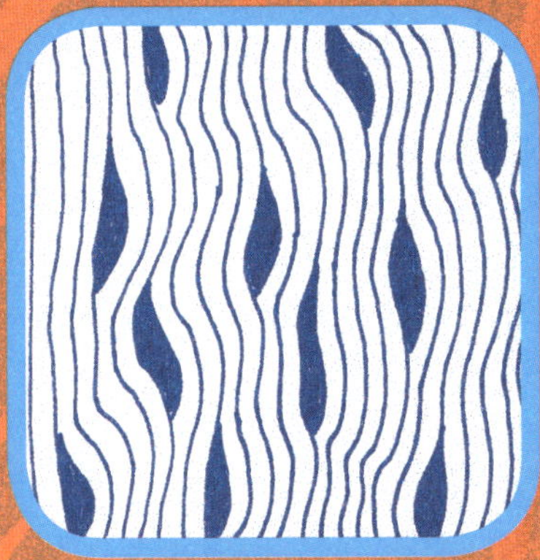

Beautiful Shell

Have lots of fun creating a tangly texture for this gorgeous seashell.

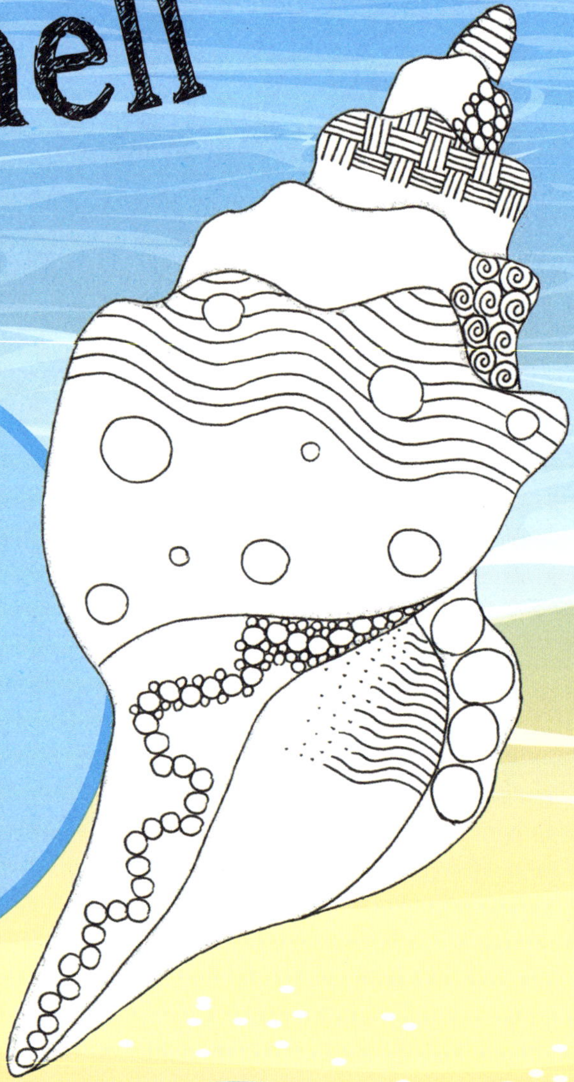

1. Draw the outlines of your tangles. From the top, I've used: Zinger (p45), Tipple (p7), Keeko (p9), Printemps (p26), Nipa (p8), Quipple (p41), Msst (p48), and Onamato (p12).

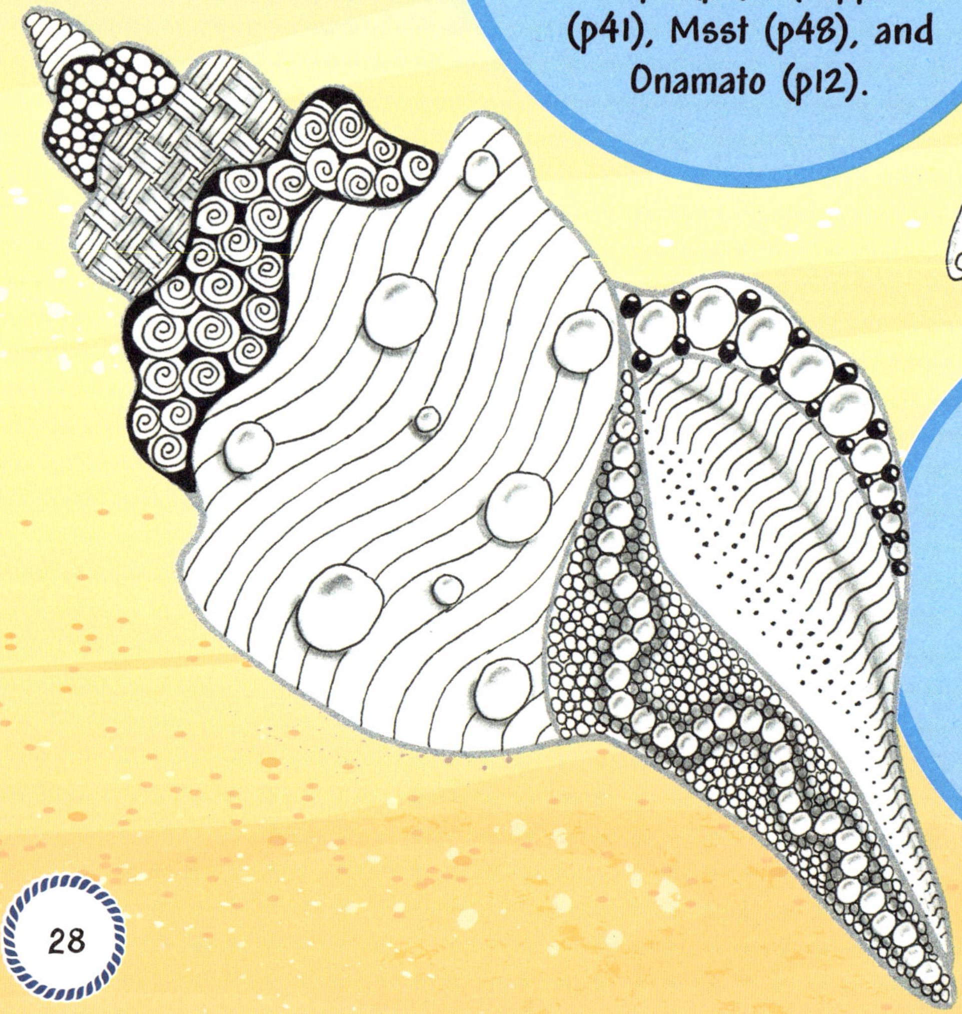

2. Add some shade to your tangles to finish the picture. I've used a black pen to fill in the space around Tipple and Printemps, to draw attention to the structure of the shell.

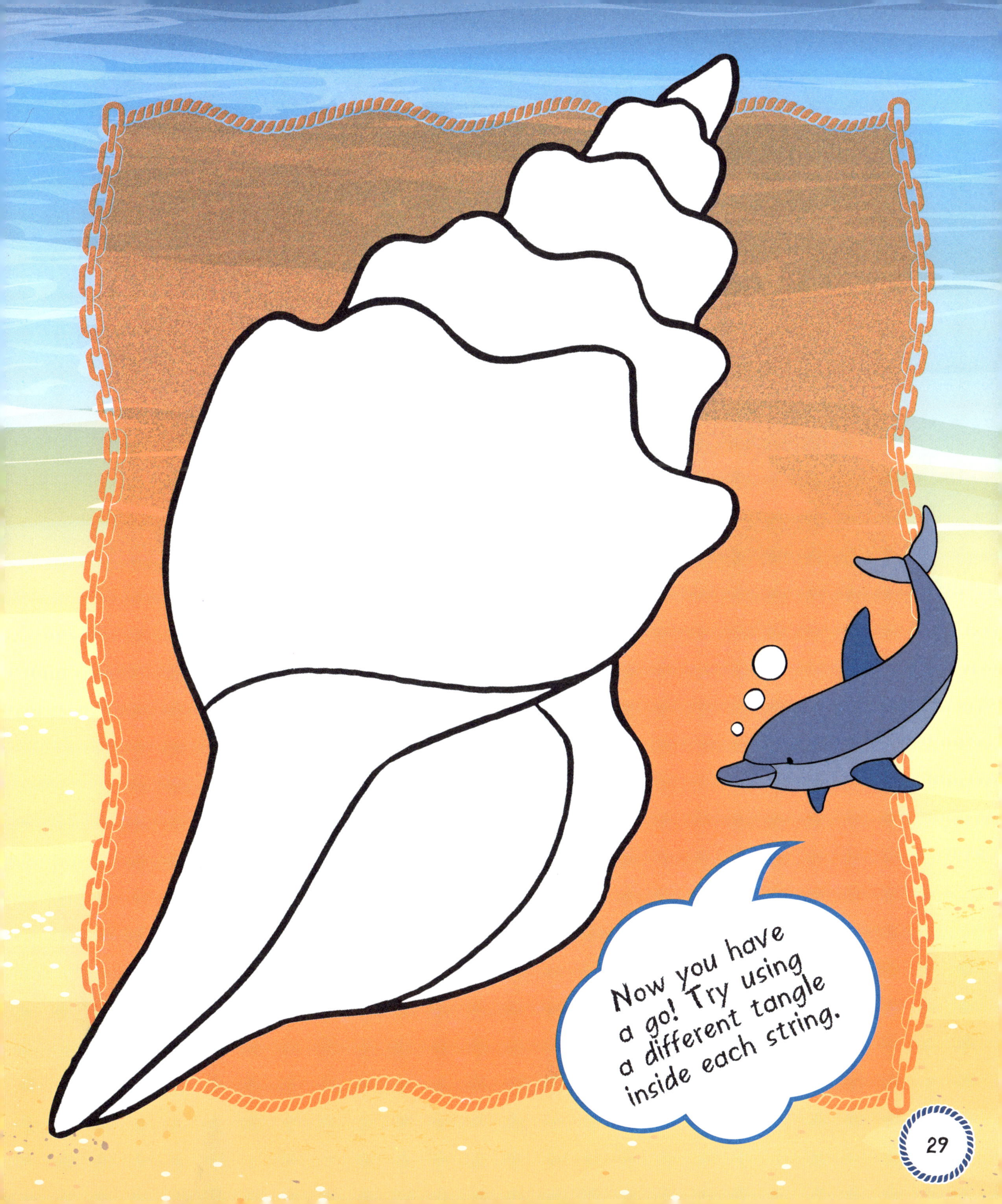
Now you have
a go! Try using
a different tangle
inside each string.

Shattuck

This striking tangle makes wonderful scales for fish pictures!

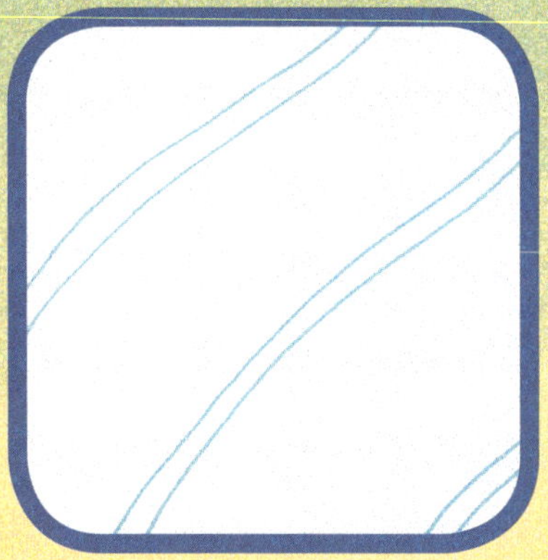

1. Start by drawing three sets of lines, like this.

2. In the top row, draw four slightly curved lines that are all the same distance apart.

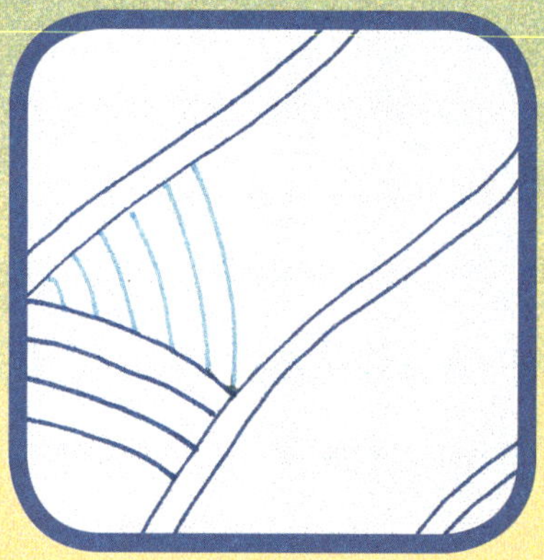

3. Now, draw a set of diagonal lines, from right to left, like this.

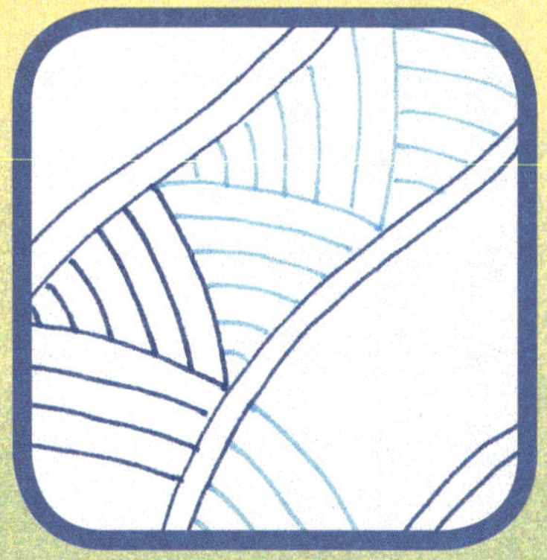

4. Repeat this pattern until the whole row is full. Do the same on the second row, but draw the lines in the opposite direction.

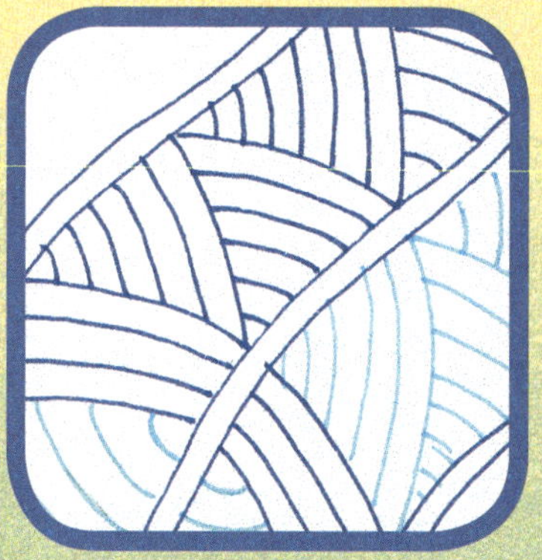

5. Repeat until you've filled the space.

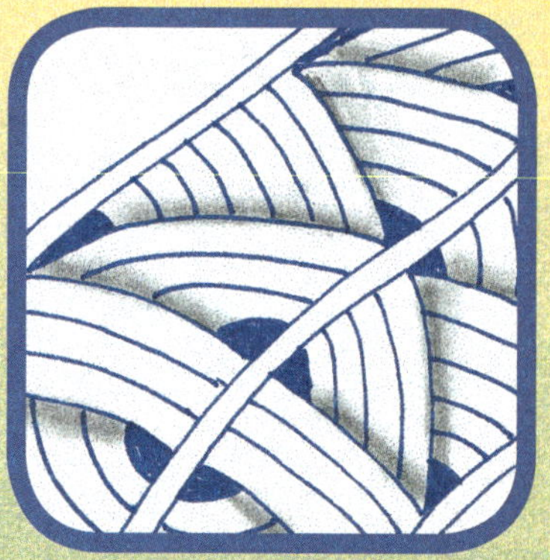

6. You can fill in some of the gaps with your pen or add some shade to your tangle to finish it off.

Hollibaugh

You can fill the gaps in Hollibaugh with any tangle you want. It's a great way to create a varied texture.

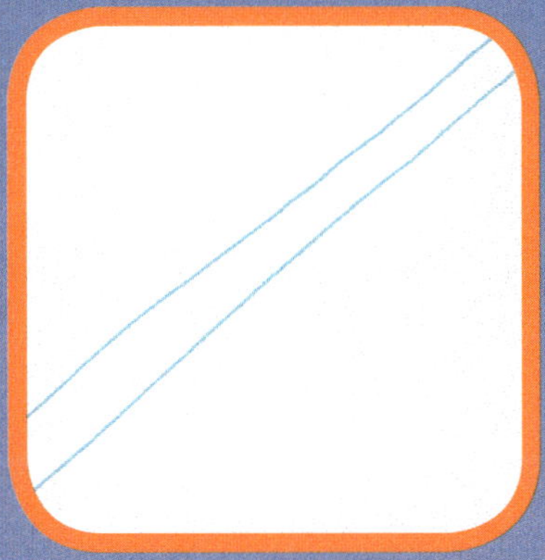

1. Draw a band of lines across the page.

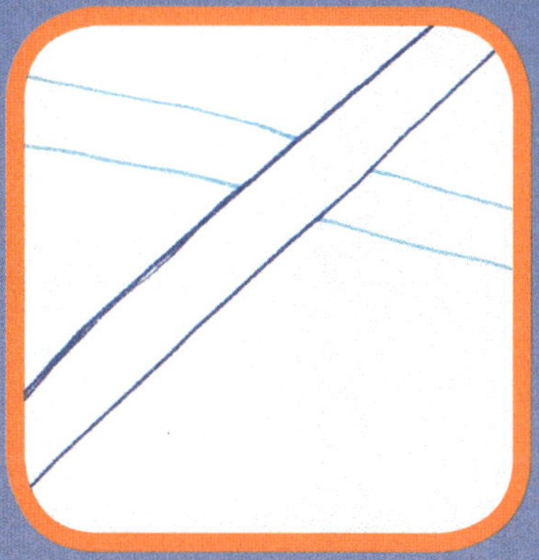

2. Add a band going in a different direction and on either side of the original lines. This makes the second set look like they are running behind the first.

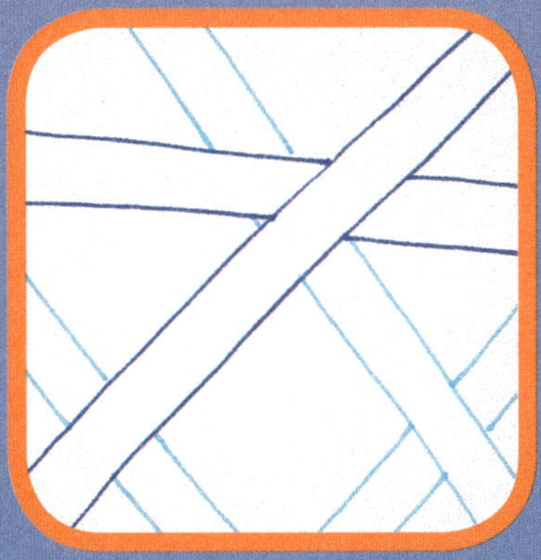

3. Add more lines in different directions across the page, all spaced equally apart and running "behind" the lines previously drawn.

4. Fill in the gaps between the lines with your pen, or add other tangles, such as Keeko (p9), Printemps (p26), and Tipple (p7), in the spaces.

Tangle Time!

Use your best tangles to complete this magical scene.

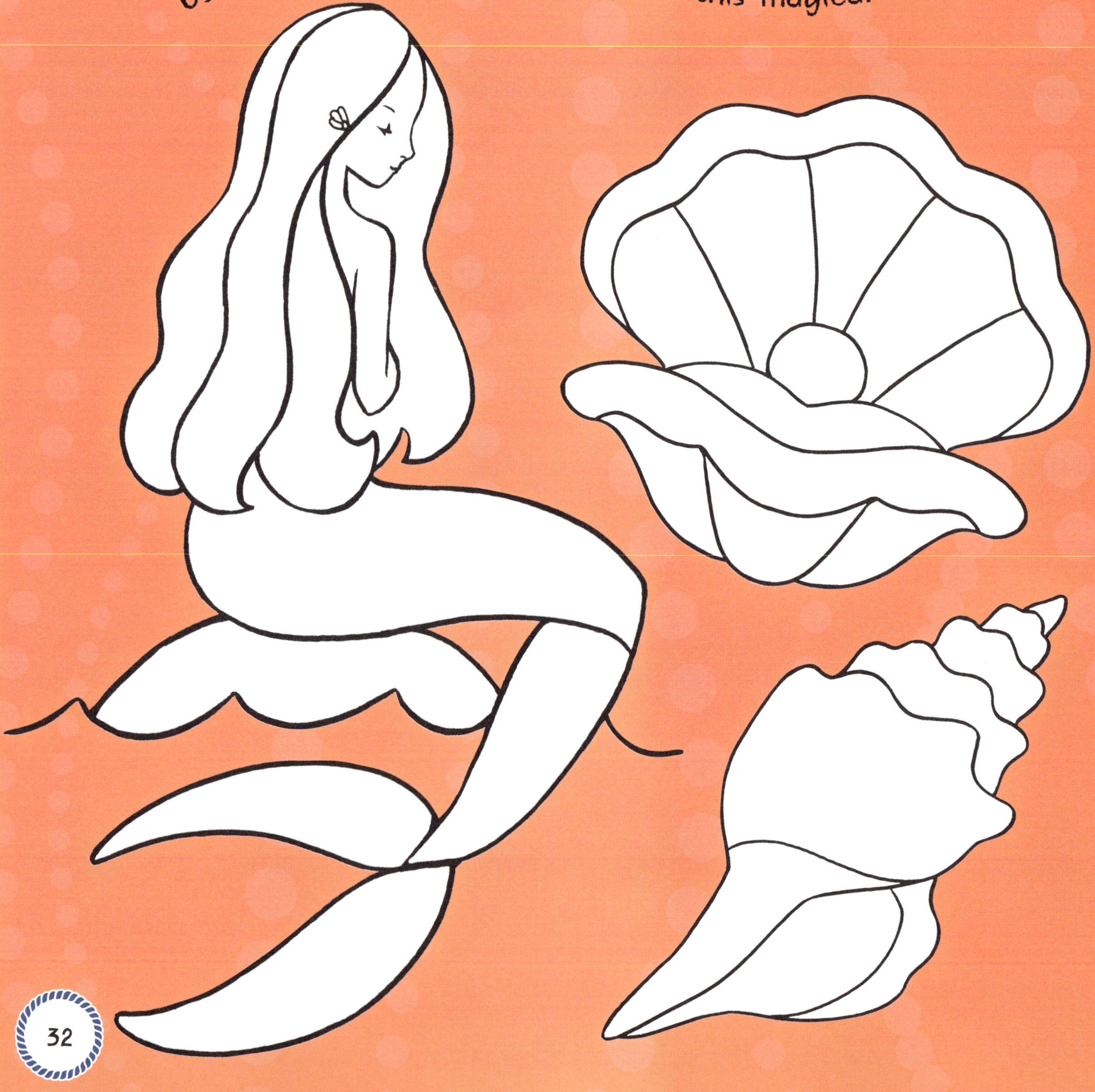

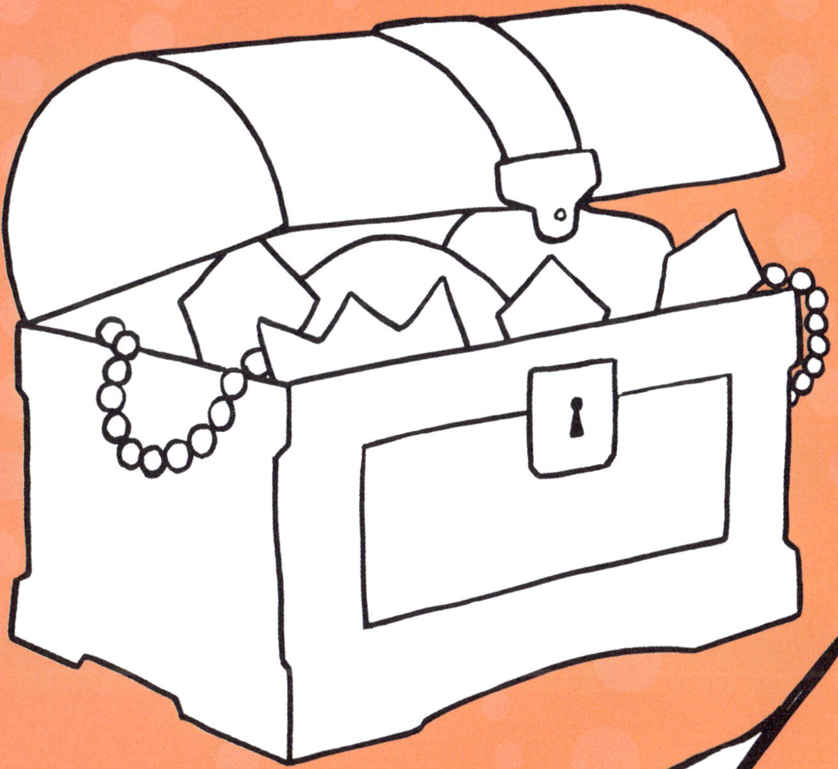
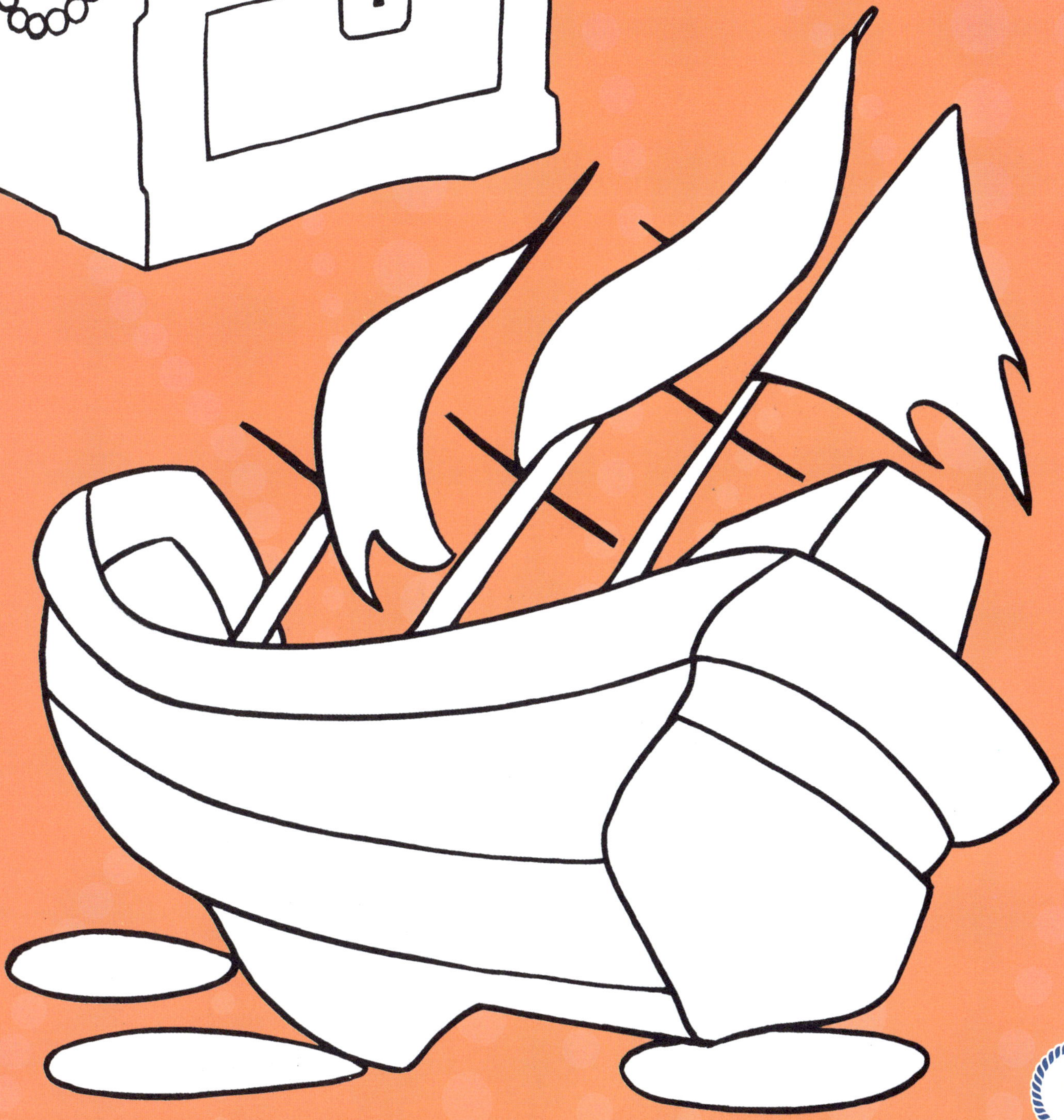

Graceful Orca

Choose some bold tangles to make this orca stand out in the sea.

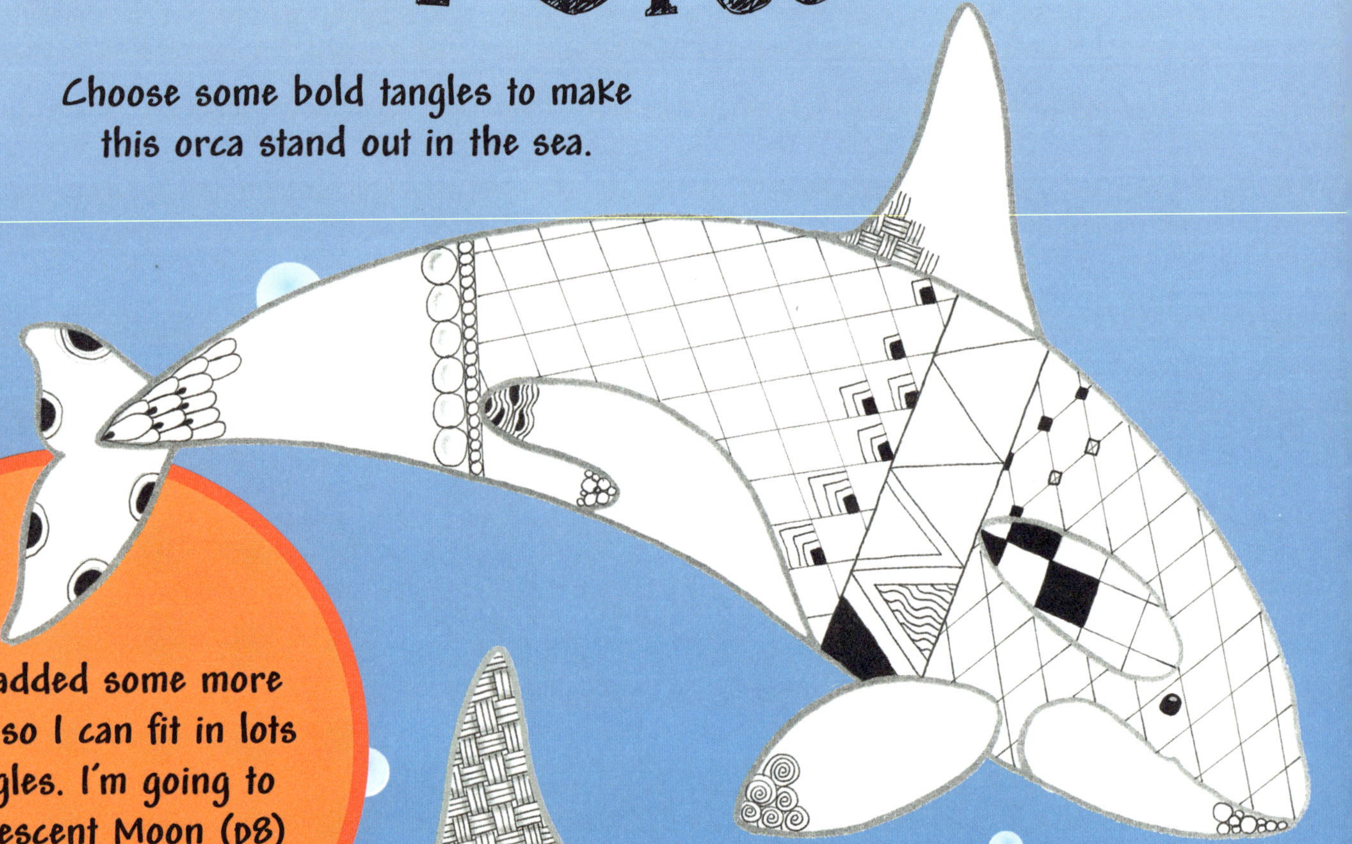

1. I've added some more strings so I can fit in lots of tangles. I'm going to use Crescent Moon (p8) for the tail and Keeko (p9) for the fin.

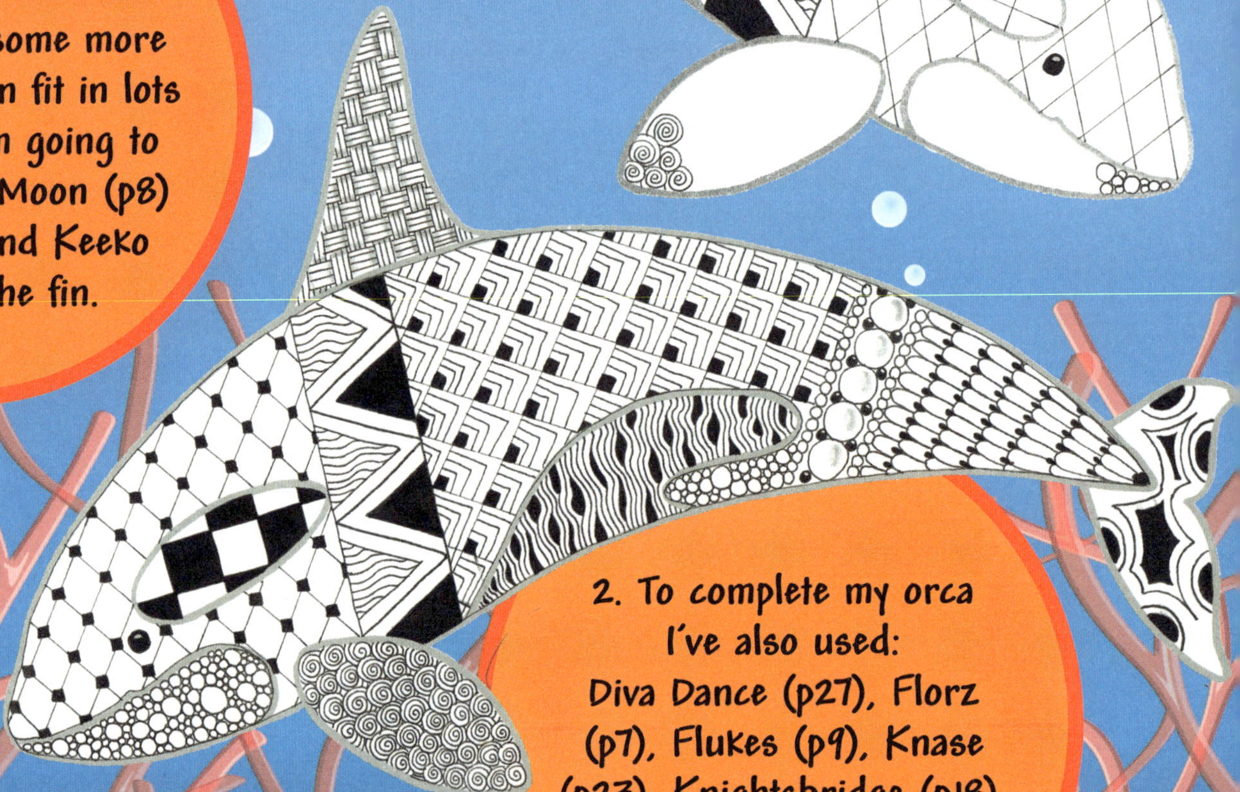

2. To complete my orca I've also used: Diva Dance (p27), Florz (p7), Flukes (p9), Knase (p23), Knightsbridge (p18), Onamato (p12), Printemps (p26), Tagh (p13), and Tipple (p7).

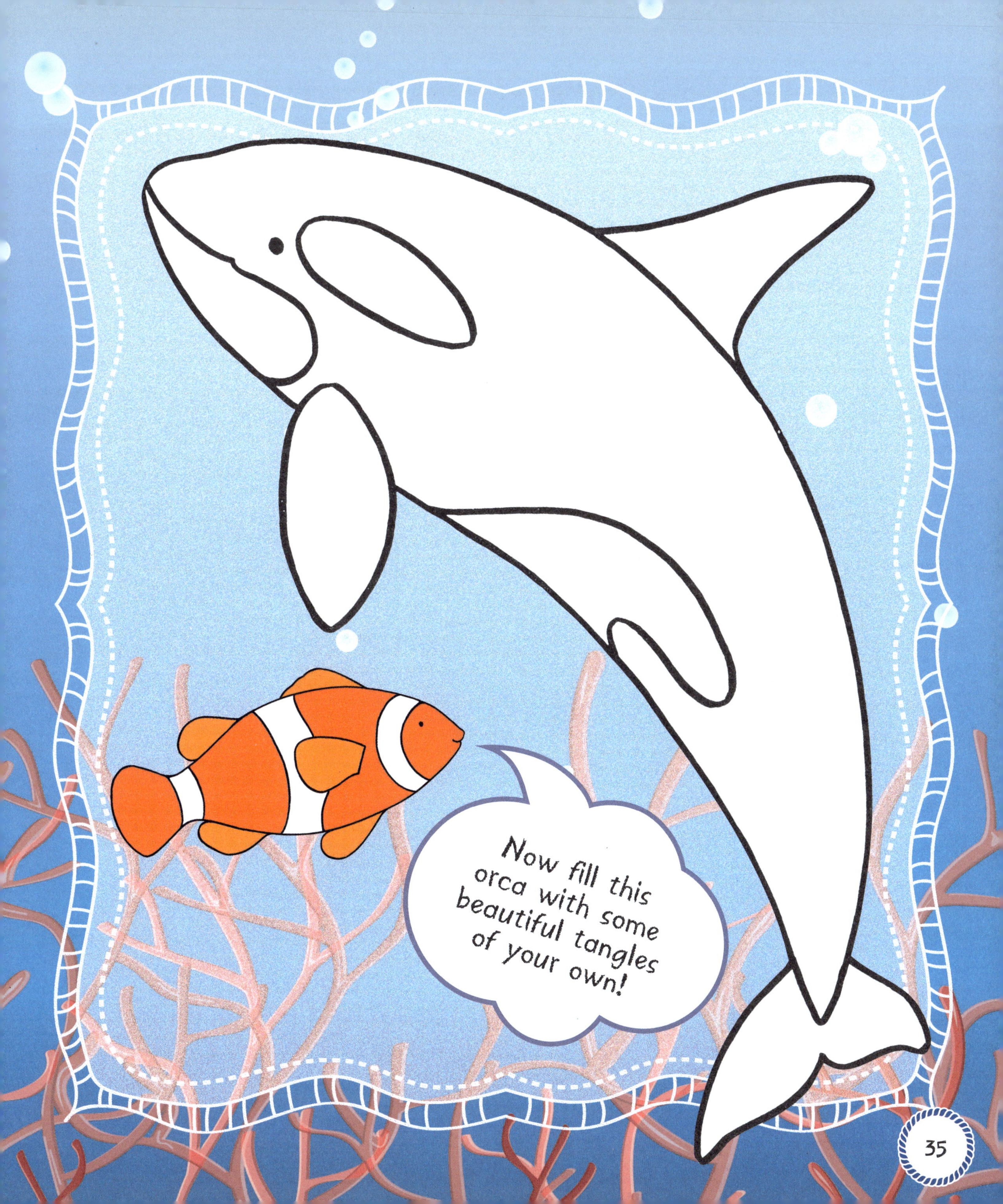
Now fill this orca with some beautiful tangles of your own!

Lotus Pods

Add some flower power to your pictures with this tangle, inspired by lotus plants.

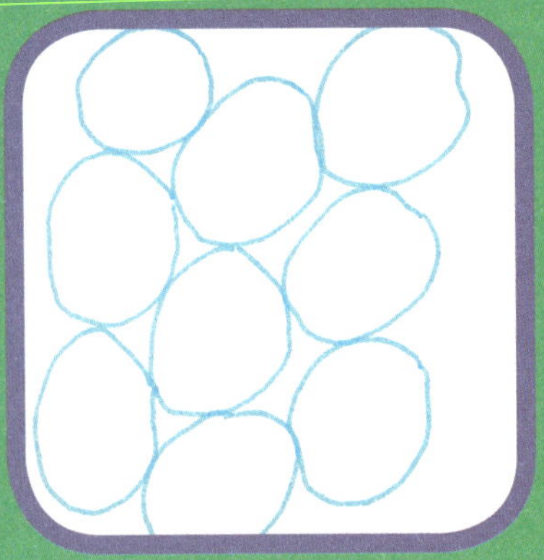

1. Draw some wobbly circles that touch each other.

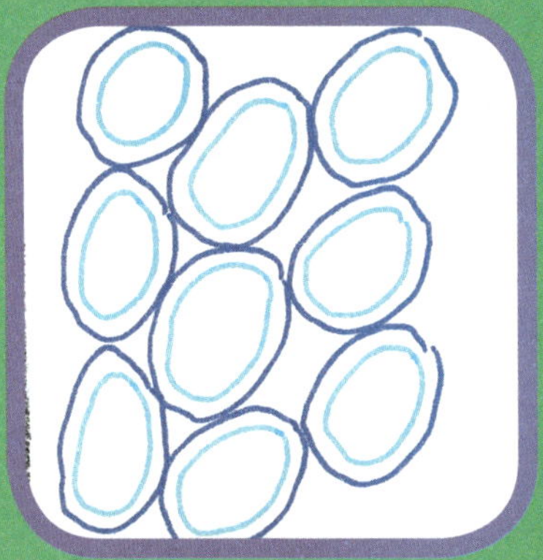

2. Draw another circle inside each wobbly circle.

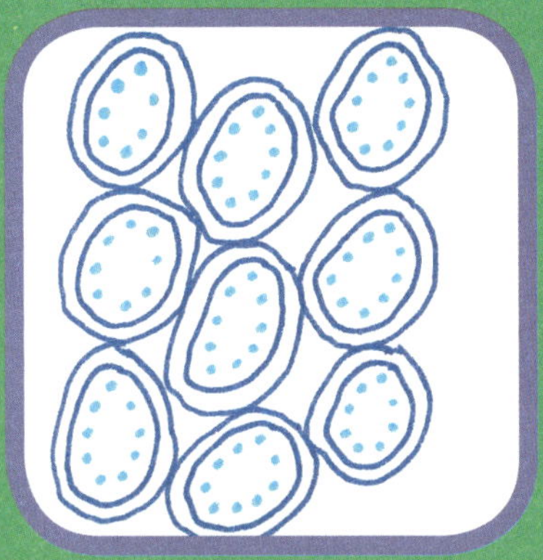

3. Now draw a ring of dots around the inside of the smaller circle.

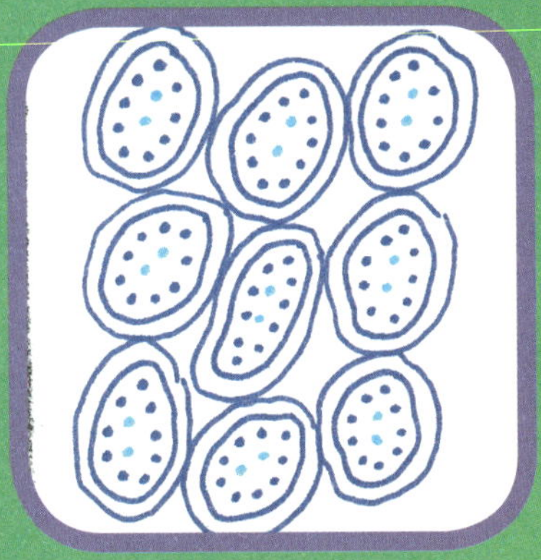

4. Add some more dots.

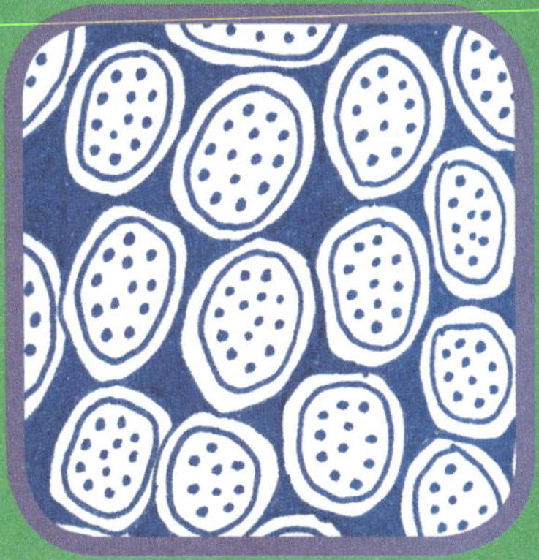

5. Use your pen to fill in the background.

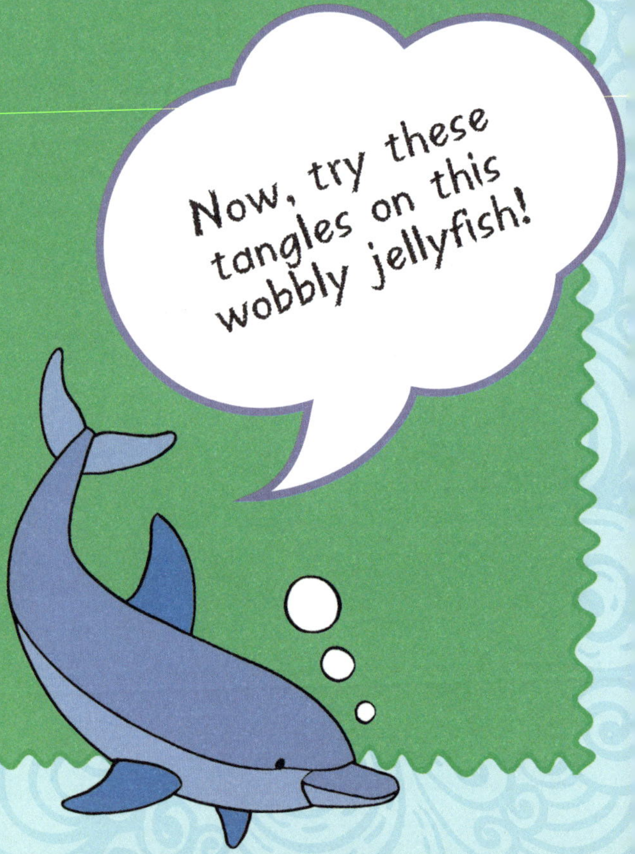

Lilypads

This cute tangle looks just like lilies floating on the water!

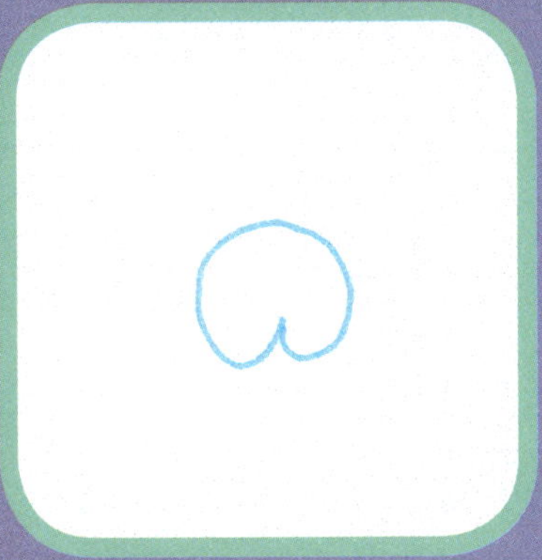

1. Draw a lily pad shape in the middle of your paper, like this.

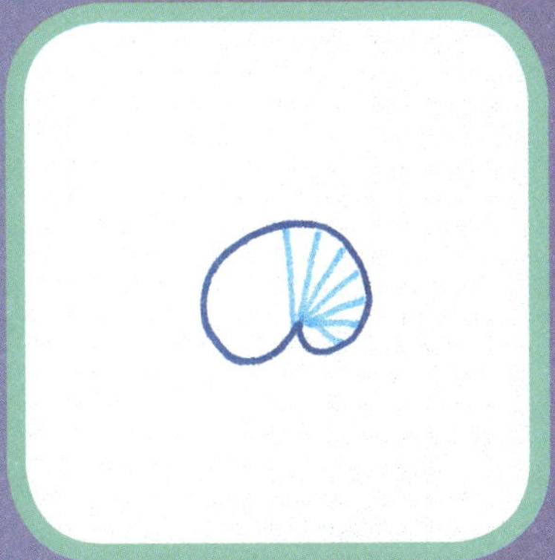

2. Starting from the middle, draw straight, evenly-spaced lines out toward the edge of the lily pad.

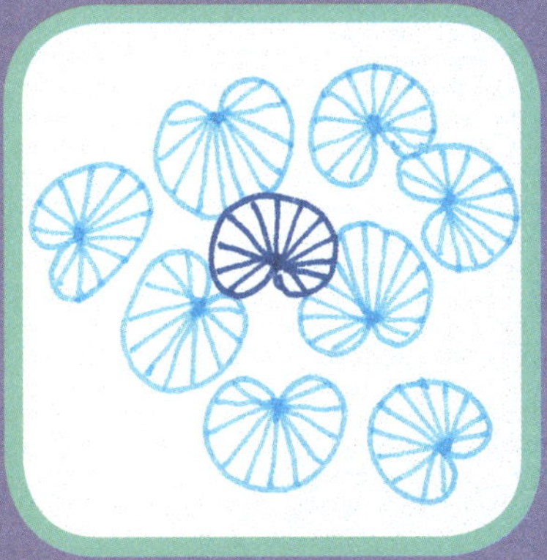

3. Draw some more lily pads around the first one. Vary the size and position for a natural look.

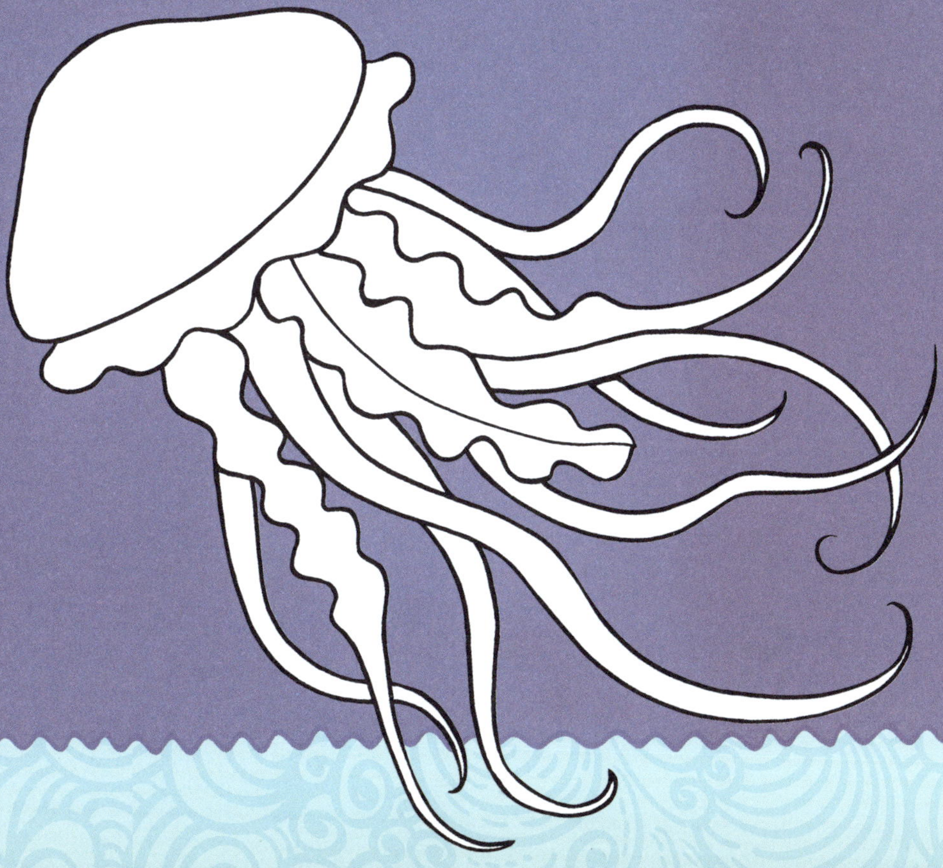

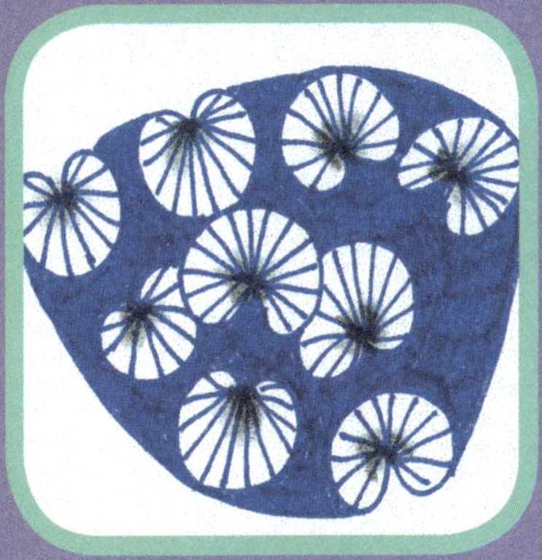

4. Fill in the background and add a bit of shade to the middle of the lily pads, where the lines begin.

Stealthy Shark

Pick some strong tangles for this magnificent shark. Choose something really bold for his tummy!

1. Start to draw the outlines of your tangles. The zigzags in Chartz (p19) look a bit like sharp shark teeth, so it's a perfect tangle to use for his tummy.

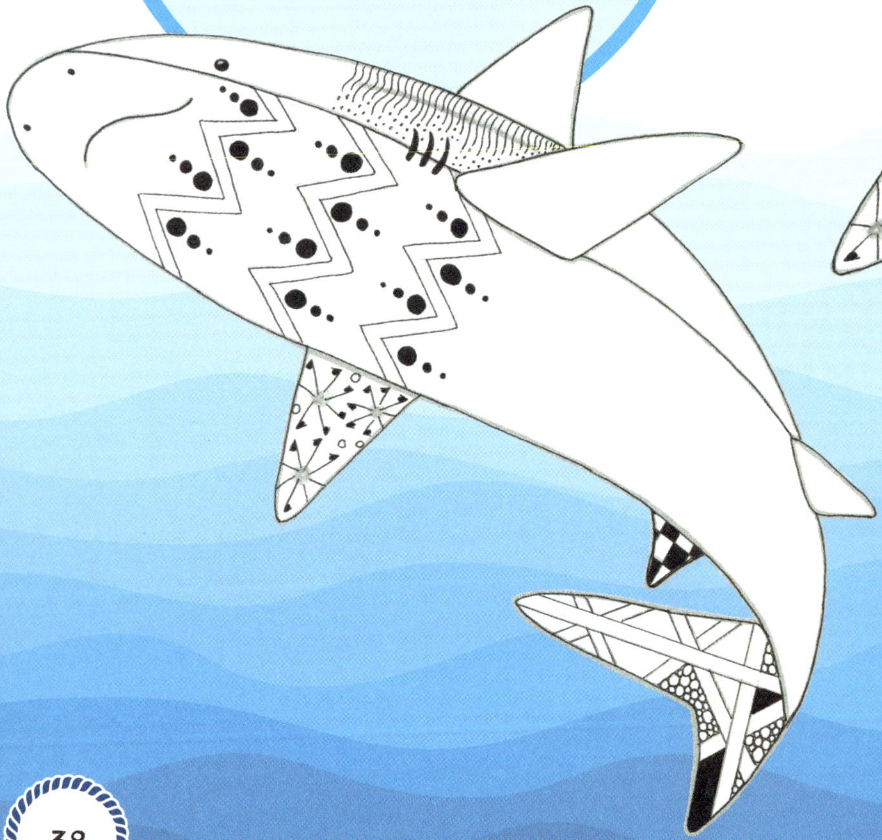

2. I've also used Msst (p48) for the back, Knightsbridge (p18) for the fins, Joy (p47) for the flippers, and Hollibaugh (p31) filled with Tipple (p7) for the tail.

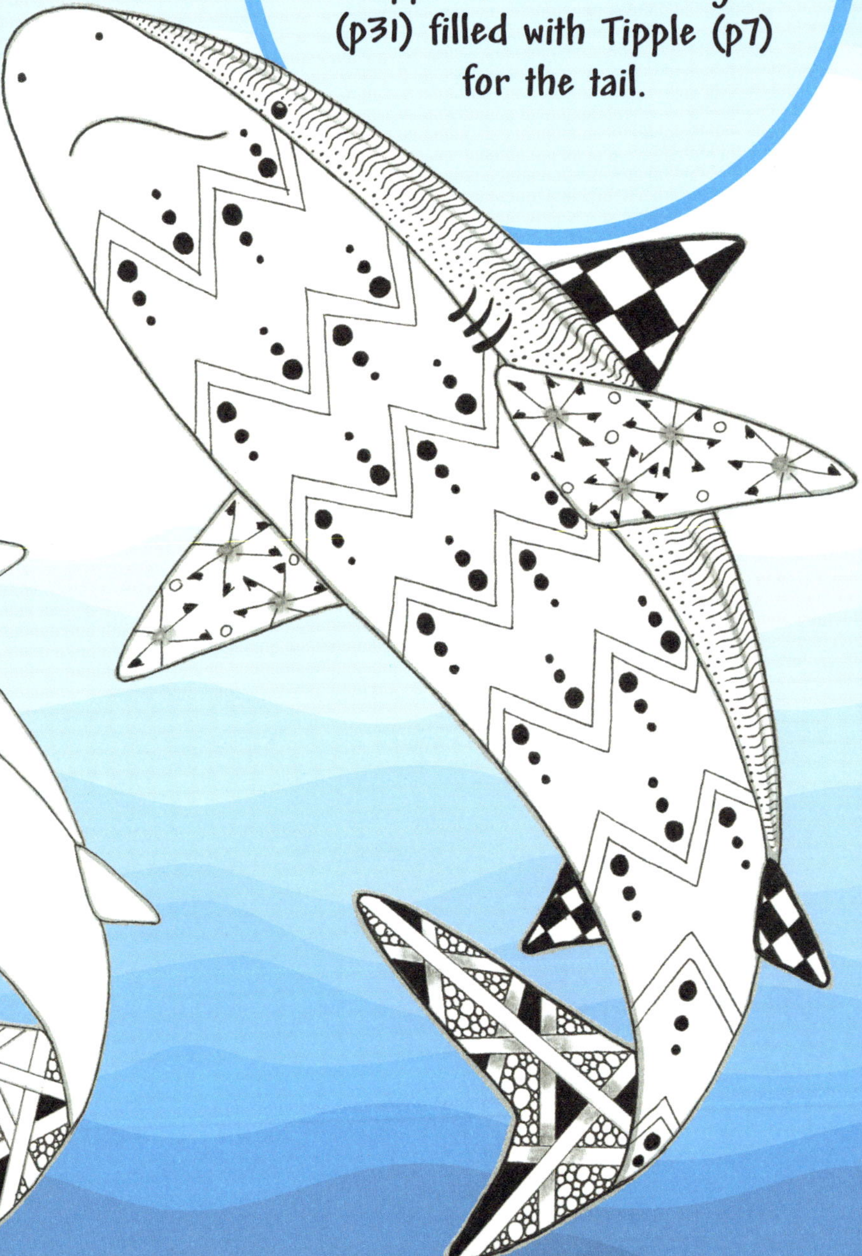

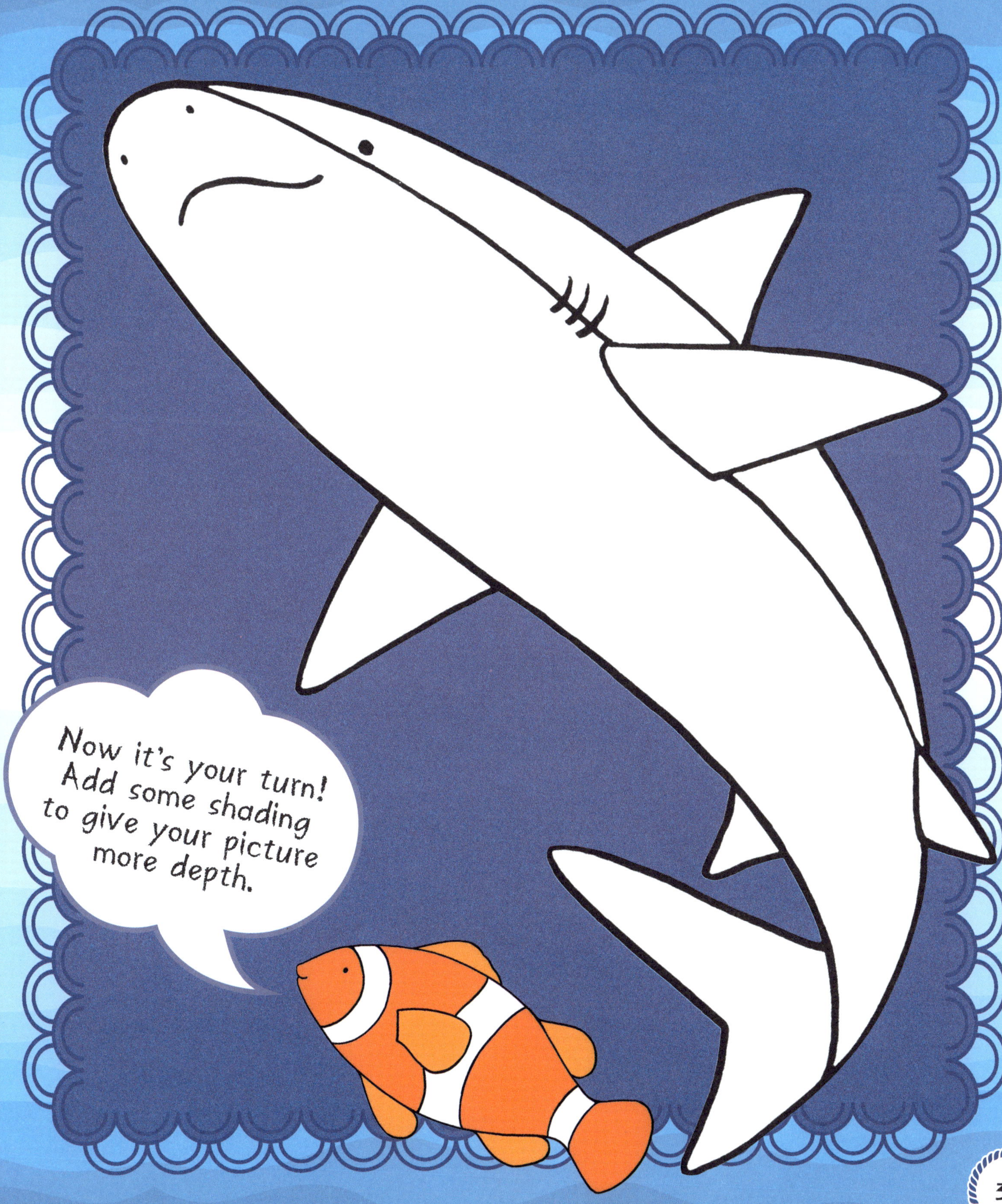
Now it's your turn! Add some shading to give your picture more depth.

Meer

Bubbly Meer is a must for every sea-themed scene!

1. Start by drawing two bands of lines.

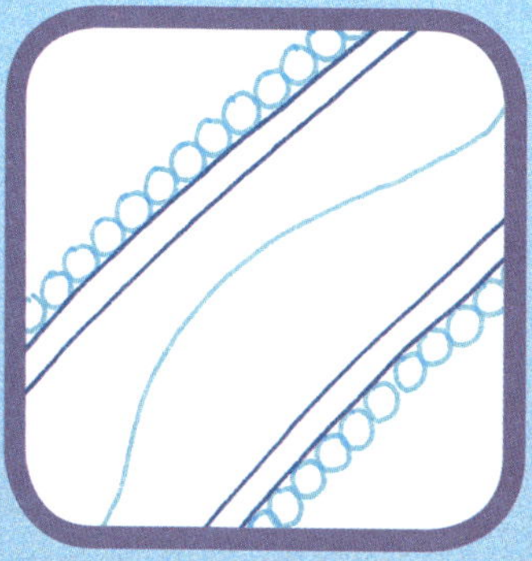

2. Draw a row of small circles outside the bands. Add a wobbly line through the middle.

3. Finish by drawing diagonal lines on either side of the wobbly line.

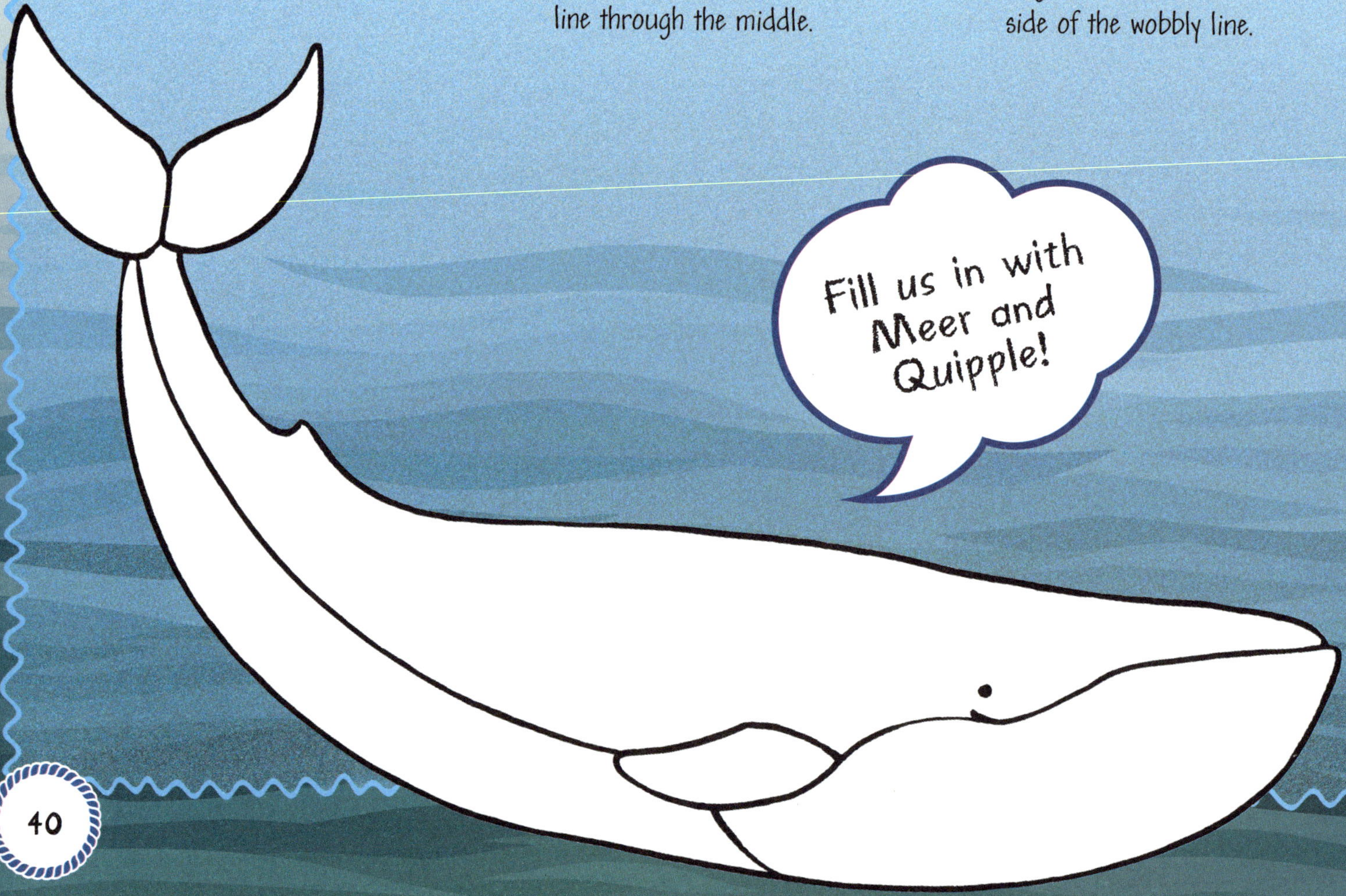

Quipple

This pretty tangle looks like a string of pearls!

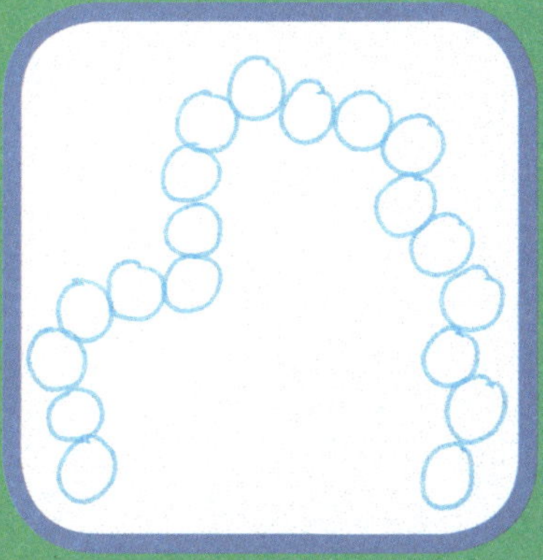

1. Quipple begins with a chain of circles. They should all be the same size and touch one another.

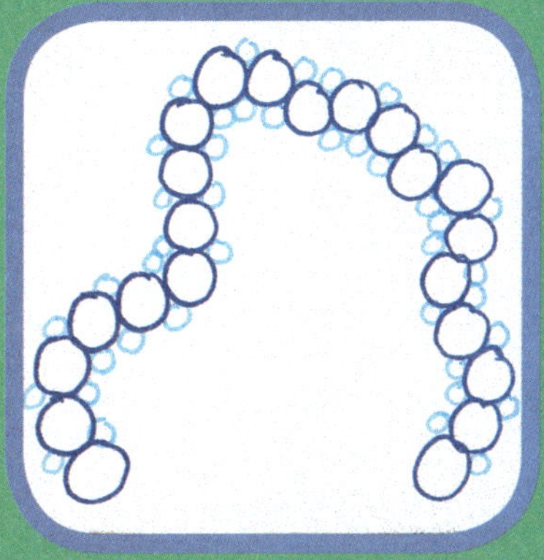

2. Draw smaller circles in the spaces where each of the larger circles meet one another.

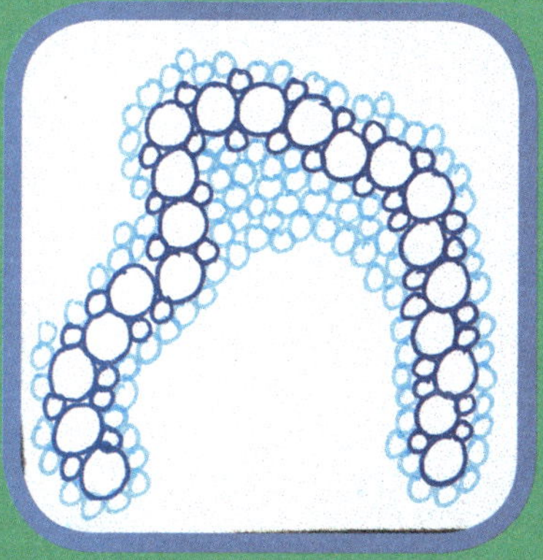

3. Continue to add smaller circles around the original chain of circles.

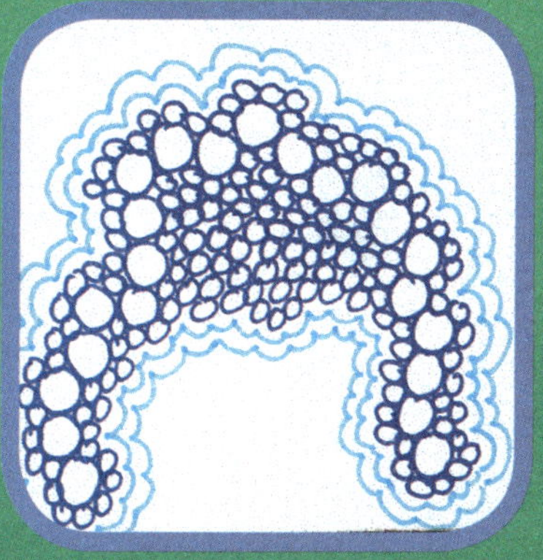

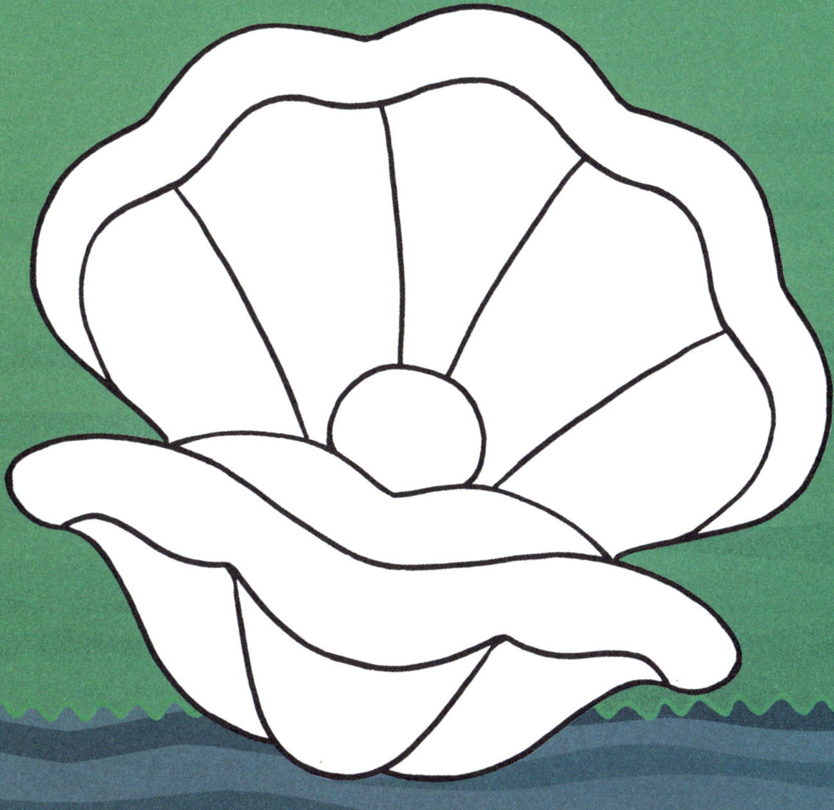

4. When you're happy with your pattern, draw a bubbly line around the outside. Repeat this line once more to really define it.

Magical Octopus

Use lots of tangles to fill in this fabulous octopus picture!

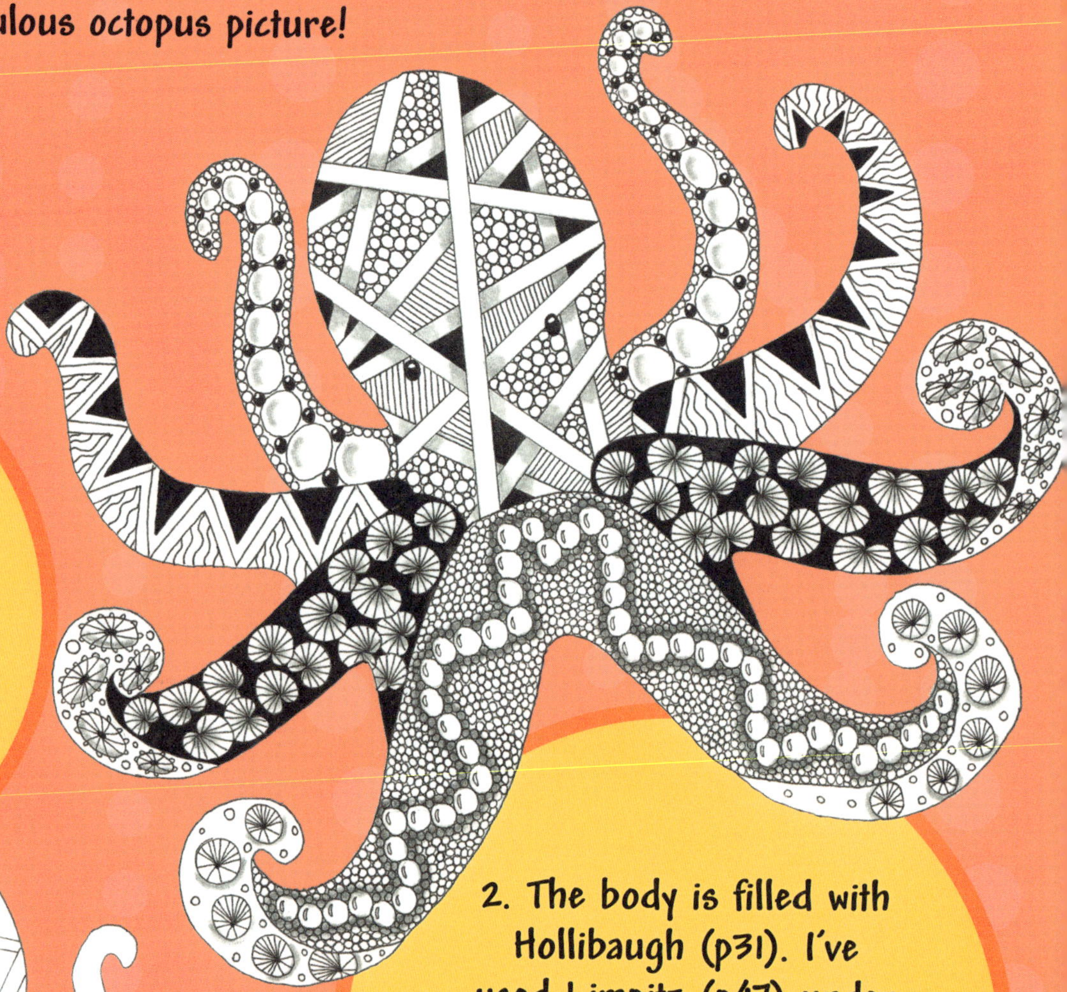

1. I'm going to make my octopus symmetrical. I'm using Onamato (p12), Knase (p23), Lilypads (p37), and Quipple (p41) for the tentacles.

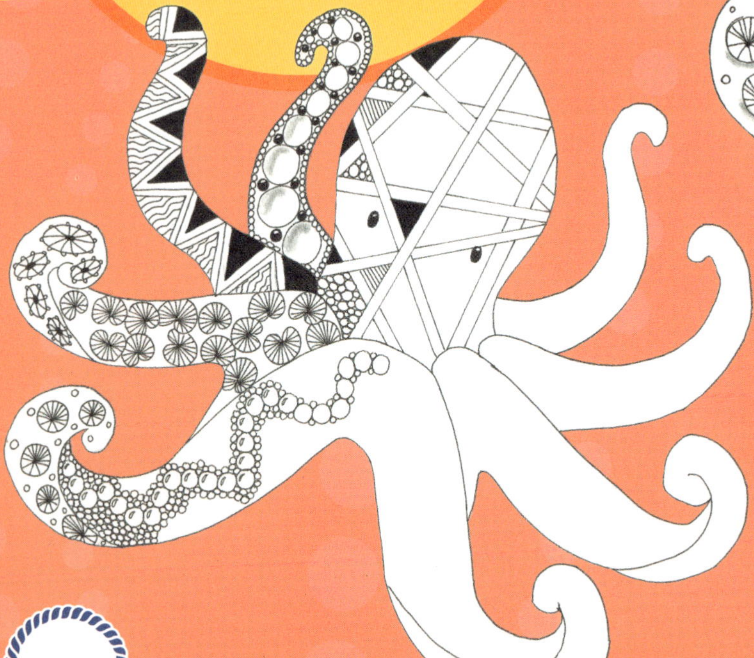

2. The body is filled with Hollibaugh (p31). I've used Limpitz (p47) under the front tentacles and Festune (p46) under the rest. These two tangles look like suckers so they are perfect for this!

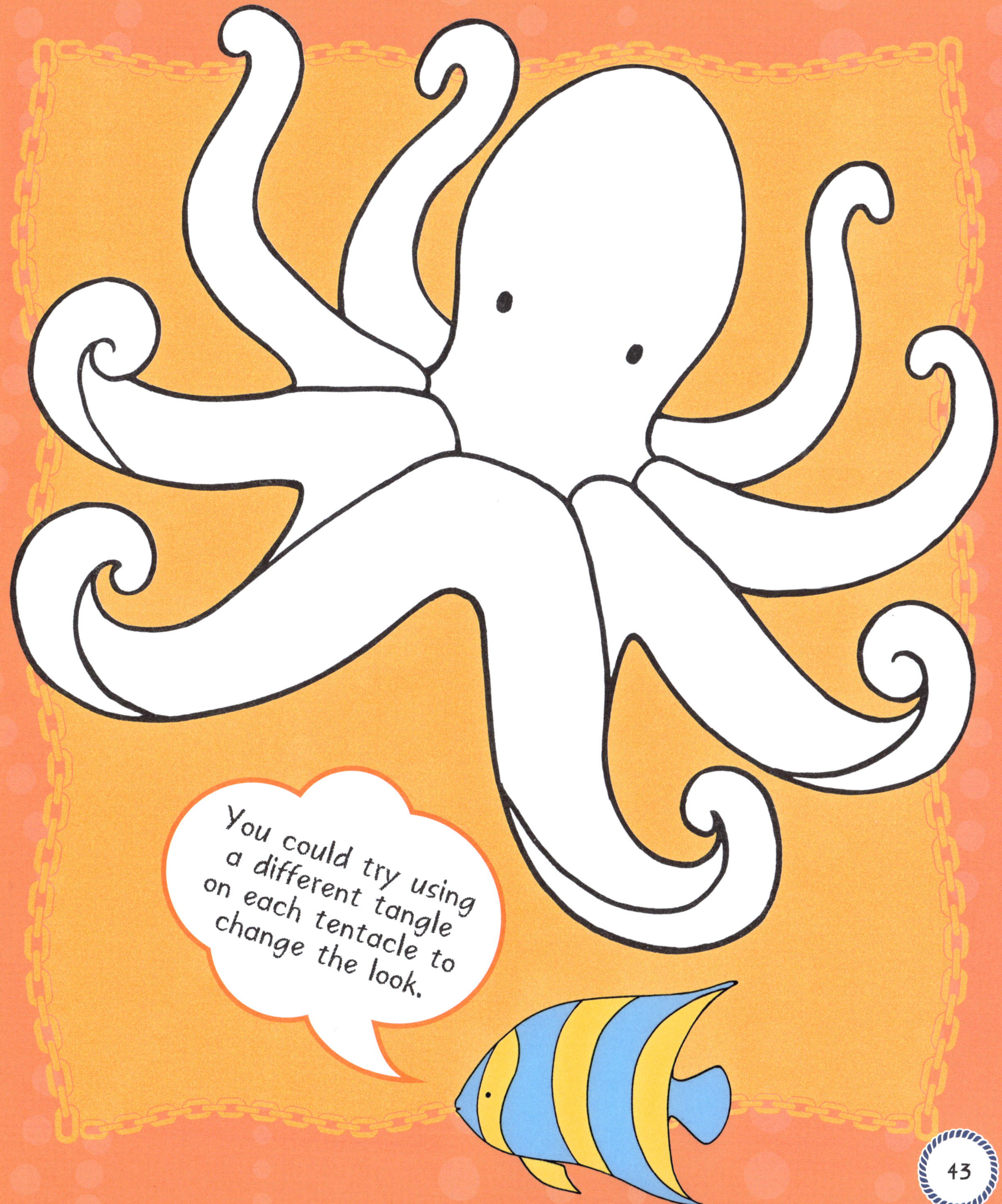
You could try using a different tangle on each tentacle to change the look.

Seaweed Tangles

Add an extra flourish to your pictures with some underwater plants! Use these tangles to create beautiful backgrounds in your Zentangle Inspired Artworks.

Fescu

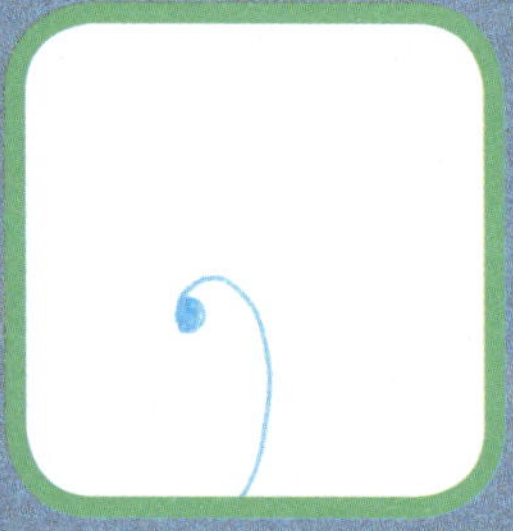

1. Draw a curved line from the bottom of the page. Add a small circle on the tip and shade it in.

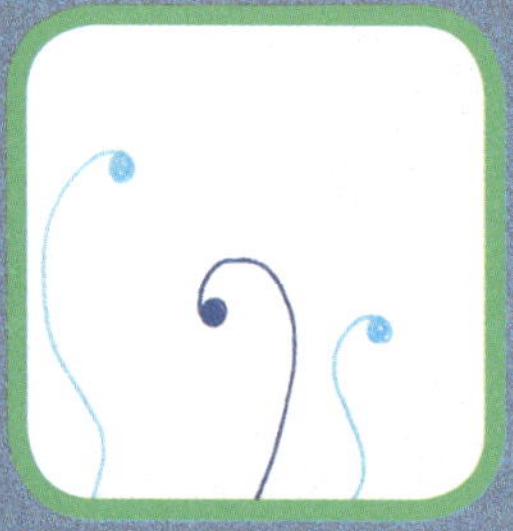

2. Add two more lines. Vary the length of each line to create a more natural look.

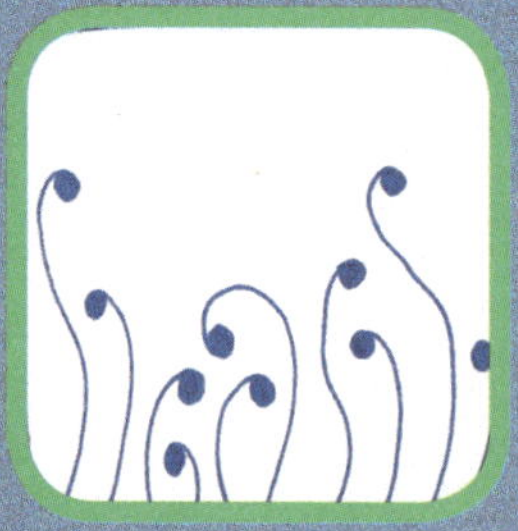

3. Repeat this pattern to fill the paper.

Flux

1. Draw a leaf shape.

2. Draw another leaf to the right of the first one.

3. Add another leaf on top of the left-hand leaf.

4. Add another leaf shape on the right, and a final leaf on top.

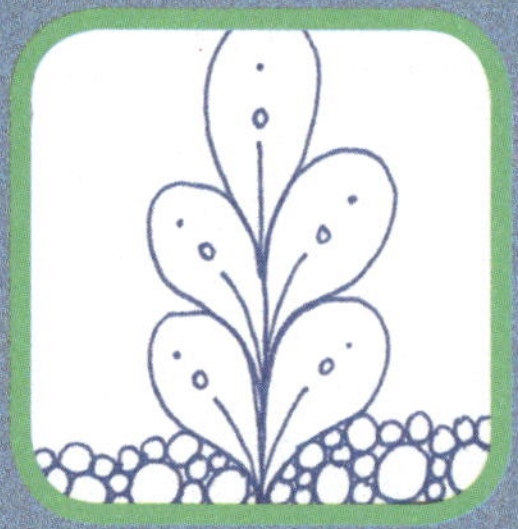

5. To finish, add some decoration to the leaves. You can draw Tipple (p7) along the bottom to create a pebbly texture.

Henna Drum

1. Draw a wavy line across your paper.
2. Add a coil shape along the wavy line, with a dot at the tip.
3. Draw two semicircles on top of the coil and shade the smaller one in. Repeat this pattern along the wavy line.
4. Draw a petal shape on top of the semicircle, like this. Add another three petals to complete the flower.
5. Repeat on every coil. Then draw two small lines on each petal to finish your picture.

Zinger

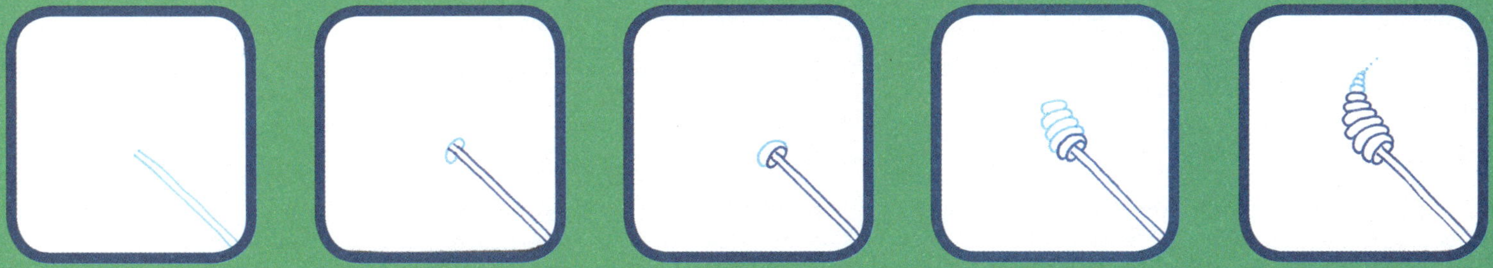

1. Start by drawing two straight lines close together. This will form the stem.
2. Draw a curved line around the top of the stem, touching the outside of both lines.
3. Draw another curved line around the top of the line you made in step 2.
4. Continue to add more curved lines in the same way. They should start off large but get smaller the higher you go.
5. Add a few more tiny lines. The final line should be so small it's only a dot!

Coral Tangles

From limpet-like patterns to starfish shapes, these tangles can be used to add the perfect finishing touch to your underwater scenes.

Festune

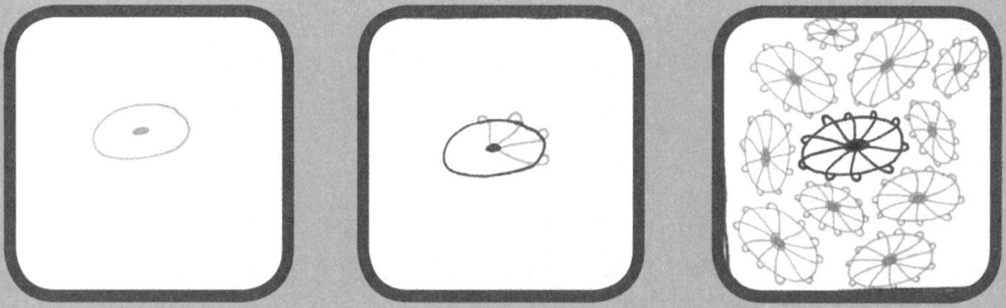

1. Start by drawing an oval shape with a big dot in the middle.

2. Draw a hook (similar to an upside down "L") from the outside to the dot in the middle. Repeat until the oval is full.

3. Draw more Festune shapes behind and around your first drawing.

Jetties

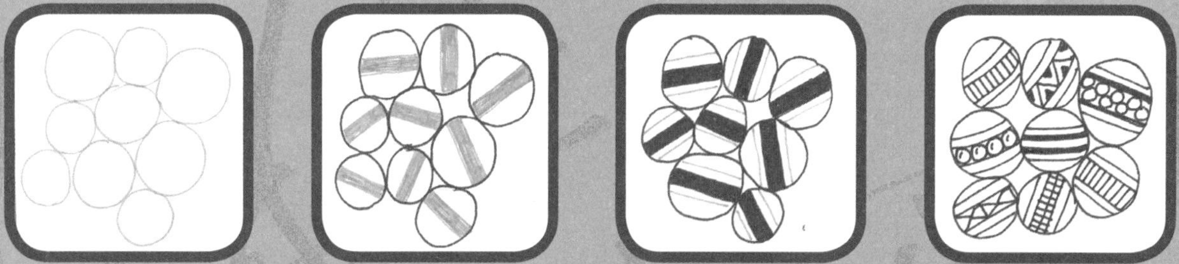

1. Draw a group of circles, of all different sizes.

2. Draw two lines across the middle of each circle and fill them in. These lines can be straight or curved, and drawn at different angles.

3. Draw a line on either side of the middle line to finish it off.

4. You can vary the patterns inside the circles, to change the look.

Joy

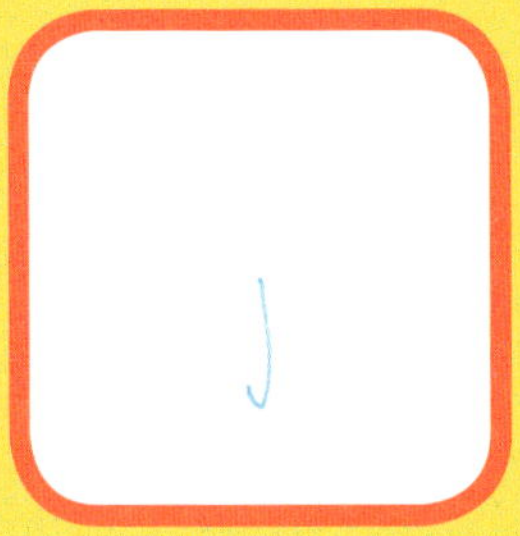

1. Start by drawing a short line with a hook on the bottom left-hand side.

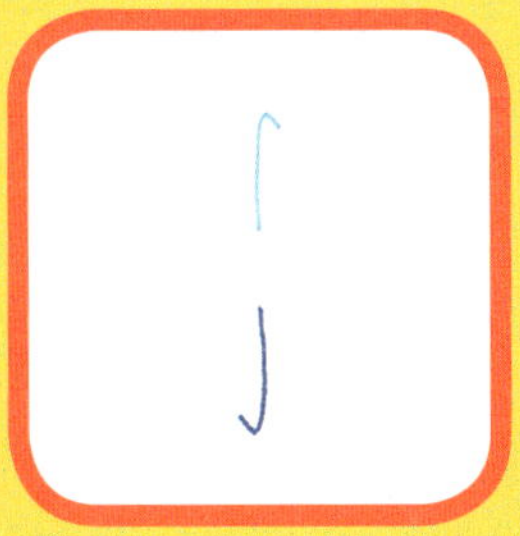

2. Draw an identical line opposite the first one, leaving a gap in between them. The hook should be on the right.

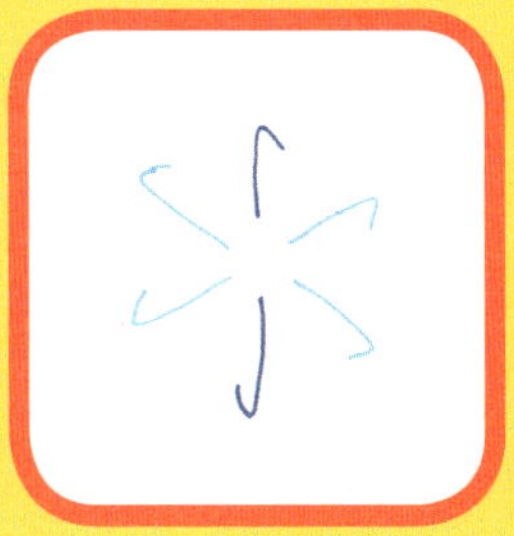

3. Add four more lines, again leaving a gap in the middle, to make a star shape.

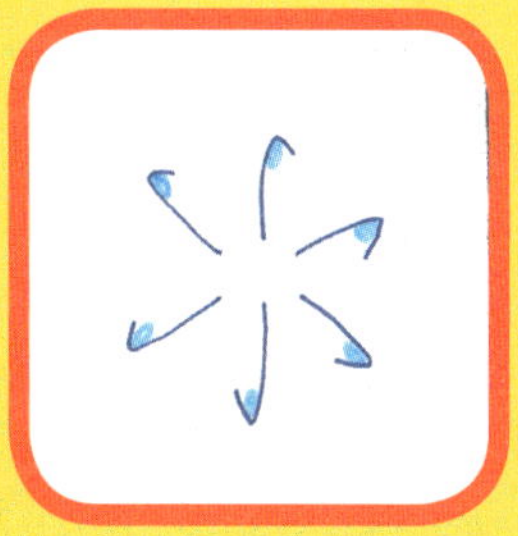

4. Add a small oval to the tip of each line to finish the tangle.

Limpitz

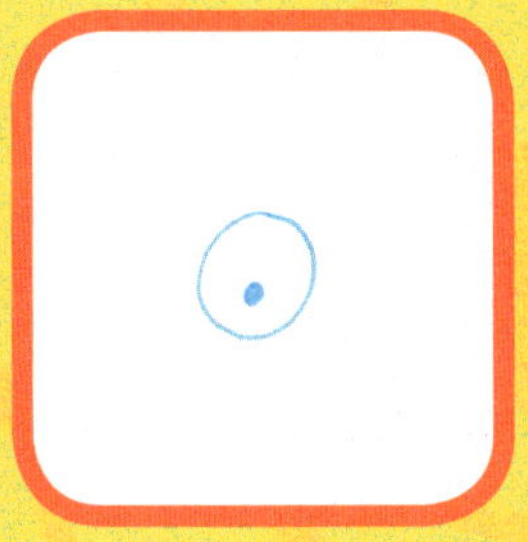

1. Draw a circle with a small dot inside, not quite in the middle.

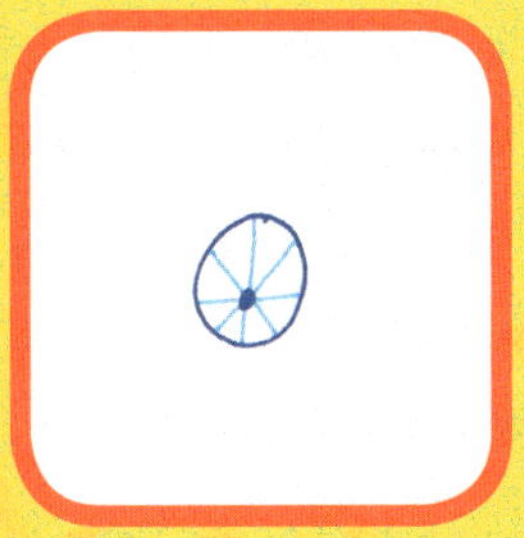

2. Starting from the dot, draw lines equally spaced apart to meet the outside of the circle.

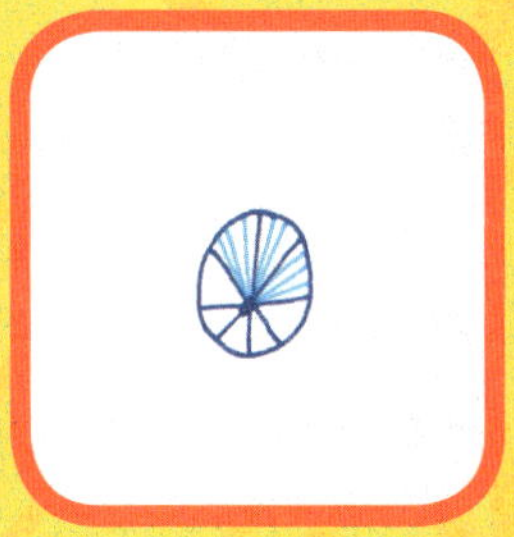

3. Draw more lines in the top three slices of the circle, like this.

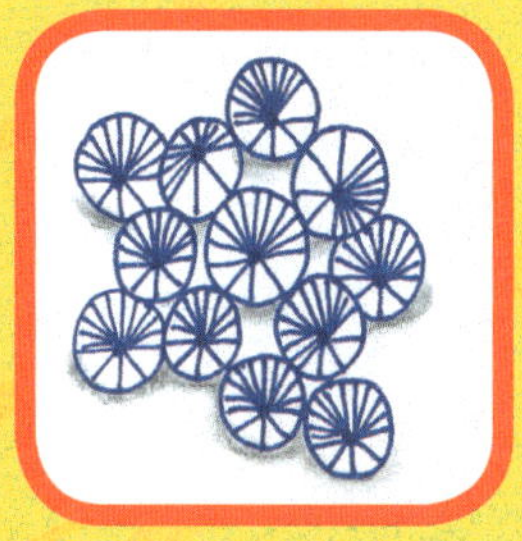

4. Draw more shapes around the first one to fill the space.

Msst

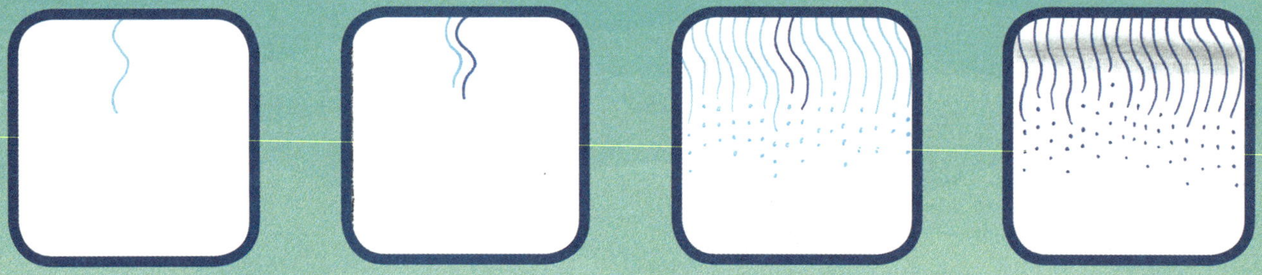

1. Draw a wobbly line at the top of your paper.

2. Draw another wobbly line next to it.

3. Repeat this pattern. The lines can be different lengths but they should be equally spaced apart and follow the same shape. Add a few dots below each line.

4. Add some shade to your tangle to finish it off.

BTL Joos

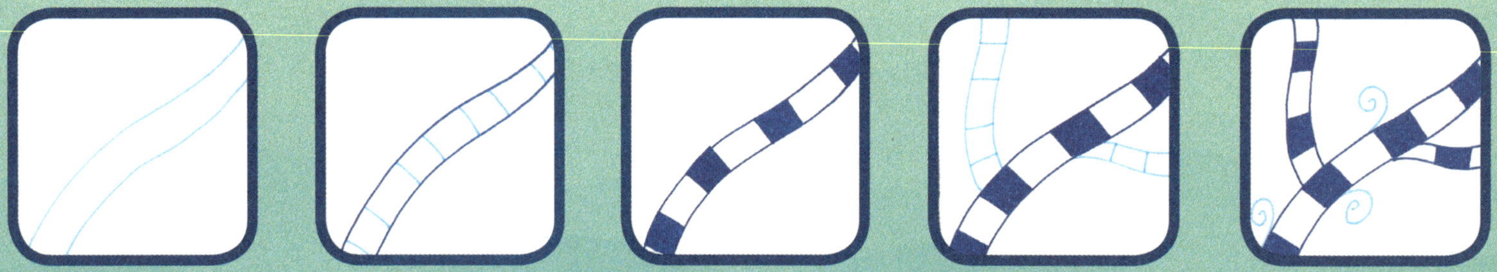

1. Draw two wavy lines across the page to make a band.

2. Now draw some pairs of lines inside the band. They should be evenly spaced apart from one other.

3. Use your pen to fill inside each set of lines.

4. Add more wavy lines coming off the first pair. Draw sets of lines inside them as well.

5. Fill in the pattern. Add little coils on the outside to finish it off.